IN THE *Beautiful* COUNTRY

THE Beautiful COUNTRY

JANE KUO

Quill Tree Books
An Imprint of HarperCollins Publishers

ISBN 978-0-06-311898-0

Typography by David Curtis
22 23 24 25 26   SB   10 9 8 7 6 5 4 3 2 1
❖
First Edition

for the girl
and others like her

Part One

Leaving

September 15, 1980

I am leaving the only home
I've ever known.

I'm just not sure when.
Already, Ma and I have started packing.
We look at every single item and decide
if it goes in the suitcase,
the trash can,
or the giveaway pile.

Ma says,
Ai Shi, let's not bring any toys.
You're getting to be a little
too old for that,
don't you think?

I'm ten.
Sometimes I still talk to my favorite doll.

Sometimes I still play dress-up.
But I don't say anything.

Lately, Ma has two grooves
of worry etched on her forehead
and I don't want to upset her.

So I place my dolls
and all my dress-up clothes
in the giveaway pile,
telling myself that where we're going,
there will be no need to play pretend.

Lucky

The week before he left,
we had one last goodbye party.

The living room filled
with the sweet and sour smell of beer.
I sat next to him as he chatted with friends.
And they kept saying,
You're so lucky.

It was dark out and time for bed
but I didn't want to go.
I stayed with him for as long as I could.
He'll be gone soon enough.

A few days later,
Ba left for the *beautiful country*,
the Chinese name for America.

His paperwork to immigrate
was approved first,
so he went by himself.
That was eighty days ago.

Now Ma and I wait
for our paperwork to be approved.
It could take a few more weeks
or months.

I try not to ask Ma,
How much longer?

Because when I ask,
all she says is,
Another week or so.

She's been saying that for a while now.

Collection

Day eighty-five,
Ma is collecting memories.

We go to her favorite food stand
and sit hunched over bowls of noodles, slurping.
We stay up late scouring the night market
for oysters as small as fingernails.
She keeps telling me, *Remember.*

I try.

I listen to the electric buzz of cicadas
calling out to one another.
I feel the crunch of cuttlefish and basil
on my teeth.
I close my eyes and concentrate
on the lingering whisper of salt
after eating a handful of garlicky fried peanuts.

She keeps telling me
I'm going to miss this place
and the people,
my cousins, aunts, uncles,
A Gong and A Ma.

I think she's mostly talking to herself.
I don't know what it means to miss a place.
This is the only place I've known.

And right now,
the only person I miss is Ba.

So I hold on to an old memory.
Before Ba left, I asked for
one last trip to the beach,
just the three of us.

We ride the motorcycle,
Ba at the very front.

I am sandwiched between my parents,
my head resting on Ba's back.
I'm breathing in the smell of ocean
and his familiar scent.

Ma is behind me.
Her belly a soft pillow.

I am cocooned between the two people
I love most in the world.

Remember this.
Nothing bad will ever happen.
Everything will be all right.

Too Soon,
Not Soon Enough

She hangs up the phone
and yells through our near-empty house,
The paperwork's approved.
There's so much to do.

It's been a hundred days.

She buys two plane tickets
to Los Angeles, California.

She calls Ba to tell him,
We leave in fourteen days.

I've already waited so long,
I can't decide if fourteen days,
is too soon
or not soon enough.

Six Suitcases

We get haircuts,
to rid ourselves of the extra weight of hair.

Ma's so careful
to only pack what is needed.

Six pieces of luggage,
that's all we're allowed.
She stares at the half-empty suitcases
and they stare back.
This goes on for two days.
Until finally, she breaks the stalemate.

She dumps everything from her closet,
even the clothes that no longer fit,
into the plaid suitcase.

There's the wool coat from Japan,
a suede skirt from Venezuela,
a dress sewn out of French silk,
all brought back from Ba's travels long ago,
when he sailed the world
as captain of a cargo ship.

She tells me,
The clothes, they're just too beautiful
to leave behind.
They will be yours one day.
You'll grow into them, soon enough.

Ma fills the rest of the luggage with papers,
a college diploma,
a notebook of dress designs,
Ba's old letters.

And pictures.
She tucks in every single photograph,
even the blurry ones.

She packs as if we are never coming back.

Object-Sorting
Machine

These days with Ma,
it's either hurry up or sit still.
There's no in-between.

I toss my sun-bleached swimsuit in the trash.
After all, I'm going to California.
I'll buy a new swimsuit there.
I put my whole collection of books
in the giveaway pile.
I try not to feel too sad about it.
Books are heavy
and even if I wanted to bring them,
I know better than to ask Ma.

Besides,
there will be plenty of books
in the *beautiful country*.
I just need to learn English first.

Ma says it's taking me too long to pack.
I get lost in the memories
and that's why I'm so slow.

She says,
Look at the objects as they are.
Don't think about the story behind every item.
Your problem is that you love stories too much.

So I pick up my yellow coat,
a constant companion during rainy season.
It's already a little too tight around the shoulders.
I shouldn't bring it.

I'm tempted to rub the fluffy lining along my cheek,
which I allow for just one second
before placing the coat in the giveaway pile.

And I'm chanting in my head
on repeat the whole time,
It's just stuff.

I move my arms robot-like.

I am an object-sorting machine!

14

This is fun!

Ma, who's been watching, says,
Hurry up!
This is not a game.

One Out of Fourteen

It's only after I've finished packing
that it starts to sink in,
who I'm leaving behind.

There's A Gong and A Ma,
I'm the only child of their third daughter.
I'm one grandchild out of fourteen and a girl at that.
I've never been a favorite.

Yet lately, maybe because I'll be gone soon,
whenever A Gong pops open a bottle of 7UP,
he calls me over to take the first sip.

There are my aunts,
Ma's four sisters.
At family gatherings, I had all five of them
telling me what to do and what to eat.

Together, they were like hens
all clucking at the same time.

And always, my favorite aunt
would let me sneak off
with an extra pineapple cake.

Then there are my cousins.
Summertime, my oldest cousin, Liang,
the firstborn son of my oldest aunt,
would take us out for shaved ice.

We'd sit in a circle
on low stools close to the ground,
with bowls balanced on our laps.

We'd eat quickly,
before the ice became puddles
of sweetened condensed milk and black sugar.
The only sound was the clinking
of metal spoons against teeth.

Then there's Mei.
The one who is getting almost all
of my giveaway pile.
She's my best friend and my cousin,
the person I will miss most of all.

Parallel Lines

We're more like sisters.
Maybe because we're only three months apart
and Ma's always said,
There's nothing more important than family.

I try to spend as much time
with Mei as I can before we leave,
to collect memories.

Besides, our house has been cleared of so much,
it no longer feels like home.
It's an empty cave now.

Mei's house looks different too.
Her room has swallowed up so many of my piles,
it's now a hybrid of our two rooms mashed together.
I look around and see
all my stuff that's now her stuff.

We play dress-up with my old clothes one last time.
Then laze around the rosewood couch
chewing squid jerky.

Mei says,
I wish you could stay.

I tell her,
I want to stay,
but I want to go more.

How can you say that?
You're leaving everyone you've ever known.

My parents believe there's something
better for us in the beautiful country.
I believe it too.

Mei shrugs and falls silent.
I'm glad she drops it because
I don't want to talk anymore.

I'm thinking about how similar we are.
Our lives are like parallel lines
traveling in the same direction.

Only now with my leaving,
our paths are no longer parallel.

Years from now when I look at Mei,
will I see what my life would have been like
if I'd never left?

Lonely Walk

It's still dark out
when we leave for the airport.
Just the two of us and our six suitcases,
snaking through the city in a van.

It just doesn't seem right,
my final glimpse of Taipei
and it's not even light out.
I don't want this to be
my last memory of the city.

Sometimes we don't get to choose
how we say goodbye.

Friends and relatives meet us at the airport
for the send-off.
I'm full of mixed-up feelings,
sad about going away

and yet so happy that we're the lucky ones
who get to leave.
My birthday is in two weeks
and I'm giddy at the thought
of turning eleven in the *beautiful country*.

When it's time,
Ma and I peel away
from the crowd of familiar faces.
The voices murmuring
goodbye are behind us now.

There are only two sets of footsteps
as we take the lonely walk down a long corridor.

Having parted with the suitcases,
I only have with me a velvet purse.
Inside there's a pencil, a notepad,
scented pink lip balm.

My favorite aunt, Mei's mother,
gave me the purse last week.
Ma had said, *No gifts*,
but Auntie insisted.
She said,
It's an early birthday present.

Auntie said she wanted to give me
something small and pretty,
something I could carry with me,
so I'd always remember where I came from.

After

The plane is this in-between place.
I step on in Taiwan.
I will step off in America,
my *happily ever after* place.

For the longest time,
I've dreamed of white picket fences
and avocado trees,
surfers and pizza,
Cadillacs and the Hollywood sign.

But what will
happily ever after
look like in an apartment,
or at a store,
or at school when I hardly know English?

What happens after *happily ever after*?

I don't know what happens.

I just want to go home.

And I realize,

I don't even know where home is.

Part Two

What I
Didn't Know

Nothing Has Changed

I see his eyes first.
And when he sees us,
his face widens into a smile full of teeth.

I run to him.
The three of us,
we take turns saying,
I've missed you.
I love you.

Ba's the same,
nothing has changed
even after three months by himself in America.

Nothing Else
Is the Same

Yesterday,
we arrived at one airport in a van.
Now we leave in a van.

Different time zone,
different country,
and Ba is with us.
Nothing else is the same,
except for the six suitcases.

As we drive through Los Angeles,
I don't see white picket fences
or the Hollywood sign.
Just cars, so many cars
on smooth gray streets.

Things are far apart here,
not huddled together.

The farther we drive,
the more space there is
between buildings,
trees,
people.

In Taiwan,
I kept my eyes street level.
I hardly noticed the sky.
It was an afterthought.
Here, I can't help but look up
at the silent blue wide open,
the lid of a pot, removed.

And I feel uncovered.

Ba says,
Here, everything is more.

Yes, I agree,
my eyes big from observing.

Black, White, and Beige

Weeks ago I already knew,
we wouldn't be living in a house.
Still I kept thinking of a white picket fence,
until today.

Our apartment is the second door
beside a stone path.

There is carpet that spans the entire floor,
wall to wall.
It's beige and so is the sofa,
there's only a small television in the corner
to break up the blandness.

Ba says,
I haven't had much time
to make the place nice.
Now that you two are here,
we can really make it our own.

I try to wear a happy face.
I don't want Ba to see my disappointment.

There's only one bedroom
and that's where I'll sleep on a foam mat.
Ma and Ba will sleep in the living room
on the saggy sofa, which folds out into a bed.
And I can't help but think about
the red rosewood couch we had to part with.

All that's left to look at is the TV.
I flip the switch,
turn the knobs,
fiddle with the rabbit-ear antennae.
All I see is black and white.
My open palm smacks the top of the television.

It's broken,
I say.

It's not broken.
It's a black-and-white,
Ba replies.

Oh.

I sit facing the flickering television.
This TV is twice as small as our old one.

Here,
in the land of more,
our world is so small.

Slab of Asphalt

Outside there's the quiet
low rumble of a freeway.
The awakening sun colors the sky orange and pink.
I'm standing in the shadow of a mountain,
a covering.

We are not in the city.
This is the County of Los Angeles,
still subject to LA's gravitational pull.

We walk one block to Route 66,
the road that cuts Duarte in half.

There's a grocery store, gas station,
donut shop, bowling alley, and bar.

Ba points to a single building
on the other side of the street,

sitting on a slab of asphalt.
That's the store.

He calls it *the store*
but it's not really a store.
It's a restaurant, a place that sells
burgers, ribs, fried chicken.

We call it *the store* because even in Chinese,
store is faster and easier to say
than *restaurant*
and because Ma and Ba
never really wanted to own a restaurant.

Ba only finalized buying Dino's a few weeks ago.
Ma and Ba talked on the phone for days
about whether to invest in this place.

I'd secretly listen in on their conversations,
the telephone resting on my shoulder,
one hand over the mouthpiece.

They talked for days,
back and forth
until they finally agreed.

Ma said she wasn't sure if a fast-food restaurant
was their best option
but Ba would say,
This is our chance
to buy a business and the land.

I noticed that he always said *land*
at the end of the sentence,
as if it was punctuation,
as if there was nothing else to say.

American Food

The front is almost entirely glass.

The back half,
where all the cooking is done,
has concrete blocks for walls
and no windows.

The front is so bright.
The back is hidden.

Ba is teaching Ma how to make American food.
He rolls a ball of ground beef
between his palms *like this*,
before smashing it into
the shape of a thin disc.

Ba turns the deep fryer
to 350 degrees,

then gently releases a chicken thigh
into the sputtering oil.

Twelve minutes,
he says.

They're joking about how Ba
is the one teaching Ma to cook,
when before the only thing
he could make was instant ramen.

I walk around amazed
at all the stuff we own.
There's a deep fryer full of oil
and a tool that cuts potatoes
into the length of fingers.

There are two shiny refrigerators
and a freezer full of food.
Then there's my favorite,
press a button for fizzy soda.

I take the smallest cup,
fill it half full of crushed ice
and push the button, *7UP.*

I think of A Gong and the soda bottles
he had neatly lined up in his refrigerator.

I wish he was here
to see my soda machine.

Ghost

October 31,
I've only been here three days.
It feels like so much longer.

Daylight and darkness blend together,
into one long, drowsy stretch
of sleeping, waking, napping.
Ma says it's called *jet lag*.

I'm about to drift off to sleep
when there's a knock on the door.

Oh, who is it?
We don't know anyone here.

I peek through the blinds,
a woman and a child.
The child is wearing a white sheet.

Oh, a ghost,
Not a very scary ghost
but kind of scary.

The child keeps saying
the same words
over and over again.

I don't understand.
What do they want?
I ask Ba.

He doesn't know.
I'm not used to Ba not knowing.
He says,
They'll go away.

I hide behind the sofa.
I try to blot out
the ghost's singsong.

But she is so loud.
I don't know why she's here,
and it feels like
I've done something wrong.

It takes a long time
before the ghost goes away.

And I spend the rest of the night wondering,
Did the ghost know it's only my third day here?
Is that why she came to my door?

Speak English

I already have an American name.

Years ago, Ba told me,
Ai Shi, when you were born,
I gave you an American name, Anna.
That's how long I've hoped
for the beautiful country.

I remember at one of our last family dinners,
I kept telling everyone
my American name.
I said over and over,
My name is Anna.
How are you?

Then I taught my cousins
how to say *goodbye*
and a dozen other English words
until Mei yelled,
Will you please shut up?

She was just jealous
that I was the one going
to America and not her.

I spent the rest of the night ignoring her.

I thought I was smart
and knew so much.
But I didn't even know
what I didn't know.

Yesterday, I asked Ma
if I could call Mei on the phone.
She said, no,
international calls are very expensive.

Here you go, she said,
handing me a sheet of tissue-thin paper.
Write her a letter
and I'll mail it for you.

But I don't want to write,
I want to talk.
Now I have all the time in the world
to practice speaking English
but I don't have a friend to talk to.

Partners

I'm not in school yet.
I need a whole new set of shots.

The longer I'm not in school,
the more scared I am to start.

Ba says,
Right now, Ma and I need to focus
on the store's grand reopening in two days.

Ba only spent a week training with the previous owners.
Now that Ma's here,
it will be the two of them
working at the store as partners.

And I get to work with them.
Although, I have to admit,
I've never been great with chores.

But working at the store
feels different than cleaning my room.

Before, when Ma asked me
to pick up around the house,
I'd just stuff everything under my bed
and leave it there, forgotten.

Ma couldn't really lecture me, though,
because she didn't clean much either.
She hired a housekeeper to come by
twice a week.

Now, we do our own cleaning
and then some.

I don't mind,
I have nothing else better to do.
There are no friends to go off and play with,
no books to read.

The store is all we have now.

It's Ba's job and Ma's job,
even though Ma didn't have a job before,
all rolled into one.

Besides, Ma keeps telling me,
You're no longer a little kid,
so please be helpful.

I grab a towel,
and pretend I'm a waitress wiping down tables.
I put on a paper chef's hat,
and stir the barbecue sauce.

I fill a pail with soapy water,
mop the entire front of the store.
Ba wrings out the mop, though,
because I hate touching dirty wet things.

I'm being so helpful
but Ma and Ba hardly notice.
Ba's washing all the stainless steel pots
and Ma's organizing all the spices.

So, I come up with my own reward.
Soda break!

I take a medium cup.
I figure I deserve more than a small drink,
while a large cup would be too greedy.

I fill it with equal parts
Coke, 7UP, Dr Pepper.

Fountain soda is fizzier than the canned stuff!

I had been wanting to do this,
mix up soda,
ever since I first laid eyes on our machine.

And because Ma and Ba are too busy working,
they can't even say *no*.

I'm so lucky!

May I Help You?

Ba will be the one
who interacts with customers
because his English
is better than Ma's.
She hardly knows any English.

Now there's a flappy plastic sign tied
to the front of the store,
Grand Reopening!

For days I've been telling myself,
I'm the third person in this partnership.
I'm ready to work!

But the moment I hear
the front door jingle open,
I go hide.

Oh, our first customer!

Ba holds out a menu
and says one of the only full sentences
I can understand,
May I help you?

The man tells Ba,
Hamburger, fries, medium Coke.

Ba rings open the cash register,
takes two dollar bills from the man,
and gives him back a dime,
a nickel and a few pennies.

Now it's Ma's turn.
She tosses fries into the hot oil,
and sizzles a hamburger patty on the griddle.

I'm still hiding behind the counter
while the customer
waits for his food.

What was I thinking?

I want to work,
but I'm just a kid
and I don't even know
how to speak English.

Apology

I take out the flimsy sheet of paper
Ma gave me days ago and write,

Dear Mei,
We have been busy getting settled.
I wish you could come visit.
The store has a soda machine
and the best part about fountain drinks is
that you can mix different sodas.
My favorite is 7-Pepper,
which is half 7UP and half Dr Pepper.

Tomorrow is my first day of school
and I'm scared I won't understand
what my teacher or the other kids are saying.

Now I realize how annoying
I must have been those last few months
when I kept showing off by speaking English.

I'm sorry.
I have to go now
but I'll write again soon.

Forever I'll be your friend and cousin,
Zhang Ai Shi

Lost

Ba walks with me to the fifth-grade classroom.

Kids stare.

I see brown hair, curly hair,
hair the color of hay.

No one else looks like me.
Their faces are all so different.

I really want to stare
but that's rude
even though they're staring at me.

I look around and wonder,
That one, will she be my friend?
Oh, how about him?
He seems friendly, doesn't he?

The teacher, Ms. Branch,
has emerald green eyes
and brown hair that swirls
around her head like a beehive.
I'm not used to green eyes or brown hair.

When Ms. Branch talks,
I understand a few words
but I cannot understand the words
all put together and formed
into long strings of sentences.
Americans talk so fast.

I used to love school,
the place where I was the loudest girl in class.
Now I'm robbed of words.
Suddenly, I have nothing to say.

So,
I look out the window.
The mountain is far away
and so close.
Sunlight filters through the trees.
Papery leaves of rust and gold
carpet the dewy grass.

For a moment,
I am no longer so worried.
The nagging voice that's concerned
about being different
is quiet.

And it's just me,
lost
outside.

Not Sure

School lets out,
I wait by the fence for Ba.
Today,
we'll walk to the store together.
Tomorrow,
I'll walk the seven blocks by myself.

Ba's trudging up the hill to the school gate,
his eyes so bright.

How was it?
How was school?

Good. The other kids stare
and I don't understand so much
what the teacher is saying.

Oh, don't worry,
you'll be just like the Americans in no time.

Ba sounds certain.
I'm not so sure.

Then I tell him,
This place really is beautiful.

He replies,
Yes, I know.

And even though I'm getting too old
to be holding hands,
I reach for Ba's hand
as we walk to the store,
glad that my first day of school is over.

Hide

Recess used to be my favorite part of school.
Jump rope, hopscotch,
joking and laughing.

Now it's all about hiding,
and not hide-and-seek either.

I stand at the edge of the playground,
trying to blend into a wall.

Please don't let him see me, please.

Too late.

A boy in my class,
the one with black hair,
puts two fingers next to his eyes and pulls.

Oh, he's making slit eyes.

Kids swarm around us.
There's brown hair, curly hair,
hair the color of straw.
I see on their faces:
curiosity, disgust, glee.

Black hair laughs and laughs.
A few of the others giggle nervously
until the laughter takes on a life of its own.
I'm surrounded by a chorus of *hahahas*.

I wait.

It's over when the bell rings
and Ms. Branch opens the door to her classroom.
We walk in, single-file,
a gaggle of docile fifth-graders.

I learned something today.
Laughter needs fuel to keep burning.
It feeds on fear and shame.

Heart

I have two names,
Anna and Ai Shi.

Ma and Ba will always call me Ai Shi,
that will never change.
Everyone else here knows me as Anna.

Ai Shi is not gone,
she's just less.
I didn't think I would
miss her,
but I do.

I remember
the first time Ba taught me
how to write my name
with a calligraphy brush.

The roll of paper unfurled
before us,
Ba hunched over the scroll
almost bowing
as he wrote,
Zhang Ai Shi.

He didn't just use his hand,
his arm swept
across the paper
in a flurry,
leaving an inky
black trail.

This is writing,
he said,
feet planted,
knees soft,
standing in front of
an entire swath of rice paper.

It was a long lesson that day.
He talked about Zhang family history
and why he and Ma chose the name Ai Shi.

I'm thinking about this during science,
as Ms. Branch points to a diagram
of the human heart.

I stare at the picture
and see my name.

Ai means love.

When Ba taught me how to write,
he said,
Chinese is poetry.
The word for love
has the word heart *in it.*
Look, it's right there
in the middle,
four strokes,
the four chambers
of the human heart.

Businessman

Yesterday Ma said,
We sold our house to buy the store.
And when that wasn't enough,
we borrowed money from each of my sisters.

That's when I understood why Ma says,
The store is all we have now.
My parents took all the money they had
to buy the store and then some.

Ba used to be the captain of a cargo ship
that sailed around the world.
He wore dress shirts to work
even when work was a ship
in the middle of an ocean.

Now in America,
Ba is a *businessman*.

A *businessman* makes hamburgers,
ribs, and fried chicken.
A *businessman* works long hours.
He mops the floor.

A *businessman* counts the money
in the cash register
and shakes his head
because it's not nearly enough.

I try to help Ba with the floors.
I even wring out the dirty mop myself.

Ba tells me he's proud of me
and that I'll learn English in no time.
He tells me,
You'll be just like the Americans soon.

I think about brown hair, curly hair,
and hay-colored hair.

I don't want to contradict Ba,
or cause him to worry,
but I find it hard to believe
I'll be like the Americans anytime soon.

Year Eleven

Tomorrow will be one of the
happily ever after moments
I've dreamt about,
turning eleven in the beautiful country.

I wonder what my gift will be.

Last year, Ma bought me a dress.
When we left it was already too small,
I put it in the giveaway pile for Mei.

I've spent so much of the last month
saying goodbye to stuff,
I can't wait to get
something shiny and new.

Also, there's the question of my cake.
I usually get a creamy chestnut cake

from the bakery on Xuchang Street.
I wonder what we'll have this year.

And always Ba takes pictures.
Already there's a spot saved
in my photo album
that will hold year eleven.

Eleven and a Day

Ma doesn't eat toast for breakfast.
Ma says she's not used to eating American food,
even though she's around
that kind of food all day.

Ma asks,
Would you like some rice?
I don't feel full until I've had some rice.

I don't say anything.
I'm still mad about my birthday.

I didn't get any kind of cake,
only one lonely donut,
no candle.
And it was just a plain donut too
because Ma doesn't approve
of artificial colors and flavors.
No sprinkles, no squirty jelly.

Nothing.

No gifts.
No photos,
because the camera didn't have film.

I couldn't believe it.
When Ba saw my sadness,
he apologized, saying,
I'm sorry.
I didn't have time
to ride the bus
down Route 66 for film.

I asked,
Why don't we have a car?
It seems like everyone here has a car.

I don't know how to drive, he said.

Well, why don't you learn how to drive?

Your mother and I
have put all our money into the store.
We can't afford a car.

I'd never heard Ba say the words
we can't afford until now.

Before, Ba's shoulders never slumped.
Now, his shoulders are hunched over
from all the sweeping and mopping
and my disappointment.

My shoulders feel heavy too.
I tell him,
That's all right, Baba.
I don't care about presents
or photographs or cake.

And for a moment I almost believe it.

Here to Stay

How silly of me to think
that just because I'm in California,
I'd be at the beach all the time.

The beach is nowhere near
this dusty, windswept strip of land
flanked by mountains and a freeway.
East and west,
there's an endless stretch of road,
as far as the eye can see.

This is nothing like the *happily ever after*
I imagined.

But Ba seems to be having a good time.
He's so proud of the store and the land.

He keeps saying,

We don't just own the business.
The land is ours too,
and on such a busy street, Route 66.
He's referring to the lonely half acre
of black asphalt Dino's is on.

There are a lot of cars driving by.
The cars don't stop in Duarte, though.
They're just passing through,
while we are here to stay.

Thin Layer

I'm beginning to understand why Ma
kept telling me before we left, *Remember.*

I think about my last day of school in Taiwan.
Don't forget about us,
my friends Min and Dai Yu shouted in unison.
And Teacher Lin said,
I wish you all the happiness in the world.

I think about Auntie and the velvet purse,
my only birthday present.
Mei was the one who asked her mother
to buy me something pretty.
She was the one who told her,
Ai Shi's had to give away so much
and besides, it's going to be her birthday soon.

And upon these happy memories
lies a thin layer of sadness.

I take out a sheet of paper
and write,

Dear Mei,
There are so many wonderful things
about America and some things
that are not so great.

The front half of the store
is covered in glass,
like a shiny jewelry box.

At school, I'm doing well in math.
The problem is English.
It's taking me much longer to learn
than I had hoped.
Everyone here speaks so fast.

Ba keeps trying to reassure me.
You'll be just like the Americans soon, he says.
But I think, even if I do become an American,
I'll still always be different.

Forever your friend and cousin,
Ai Shi

I place the letter in an envelope
for Ma to mail off.

I sit for a moment
and imagine these words
making the long reverse journey to Taiwan,
retracing the steps I took to get here.

Living Room

The store is empty in the afternoons.
It's usually quiet around
the space between lunch and dinner.
This is when we can be together,
just the three of us,
when the store feels more like
a living room
than anything else.

At night when we go back
to the apartment,
it will already be dark
and almost time for bed.
Ba likes to keep the lights
in the apartment dim to save money.

So the three of us,
in the afternoons

we sit in the front of the store
where the walls are made of glass
and it is so warm and bright.

I tell them about my day,
and what I'm learning
and how I miss my old friends
and Mei.

Ma and Ba sit and listen, nodding quietly.
They don't interrupt.
Ba tells me he understands.
Ma squeezes my hand.
Somehow sharing about being lonely
makes it a little less so.

Swing

The school playground sits on a hill
where an endless stretch of grass
meets the sky
in a far-off distance.

When the recess bell rings,
I run to a place
where I am away from everyone.

I'd like to have friends
but I'll settle
for being left alone.

I love this hill,
where the dark grass
is so thick and soft,
and up above such a watery blue.

On the swing,
I sail through the sky.
The wind whips my hair,
I turn my face toward the sun.

There's a pause
and then the feeling of falling.

High above the playground,
I can hear the other kids laughing.
It's such a comforting sound,
so long as they are not laughing at me.

I'm so small.
Everywhere else,
at the store and the apartment,
I wish I was older, bigger.

Here, I'm small and light.
It's all right to be small here.

Pee Yew!

Lunch is a fried egg sandwich.

It sits on my lap.
I bow my head low,
and take small bites.

Still, the other kids, they notice.
It's as if making fun of my food
has become a group lunchtime activity.

The week before,
they teased me for bringing my favorite,
pork sung rolled into a rice ball.
The kids wrinkled their noses,
pee yew!

Afterward, I told Ba,
Please, no more rice for lunch.

That made me sad,
because rice and pork sung is my favorite.

These kids eat peanut butter and jelly
or this pink meat, baloney,
between two slices of bread.

I imagine what it would be like,
if at my old school,
a kid showed up with a baloney sandwich.
She'd be teased mercilessly
and yes, I probably would have joined in.

But I'm not at my old school, I'm here.
And besides, objectively speaking,
baloney smells.

If I had the courage,
I'd pinch my nose and yell,
pee yew!

I have the words,
I just don't have the courage.

Same Pot

Even though I brought rice to school,
I eat American food for dinner
more often than Ma's cooking.
Funny, huh?

Sometimes I'll have
two fried chicken wings, extra crispy,
a side of coleslaw,
and a roll with a half-ounce packet of honey,
or the same sides but with ribs,
or a hamburger and fries.
Always a small 7-Pepper to drink.

Ma used to spend hours cooking
three dishes and a soup every night.
And she'd never serve leftovers.

That was before.
Now she doesn't have time to cook.
So she takes a big pot
and plops in chunks of oxtail,
cut-up carrots,
smashed-up whole tomatoes,
onions and cloves of garlic,
potatoes and wedges of cabbage.
The whole thing boiled with salt,
then ladled over white rice.

It sounds worse than it is.
There's comfort in the tender meat
and marrow-flavored soup.
It's the leftovers that get me.

The same pot for three days.
It moves from the stove
to the table
then to the fridge,
where it waits
to be reheated again
the next day.

I don't like leftovers.

I have Ma's stew
the first night
and the rest of the time,
I eat American food.

Blue Eyes

There is only one market in town,
the Pantry.

Before, my idea of a good time
was going to the movies
or having hot pot with Mei's family.

Now, walking around the grocery store
is the closest thing to an outing.

I try to make the most of it.
Today I'm making my way
down the cereal aisle, real slow.
I've watched enough TV to have a wishlist.
Lucky Charms!
Silly rabbit, Trix are for kids!
I'm cuckoo for Cocoa Puffs!

I could never ask Ma to buy any of this stuff,
I know she'd never approve
of such colorful food,
but a girl can dream.

When it's time to leave,
I hand Ba a jar of peanut butter and ask,
Can I have this for lunch instead?

I make my voice calm
and not desperate-sounding.
Although if he says no,
I'm not sure what I'll do.
I don't like being teased for my egg sandwiches.

Ba asks,
Yes, but what is it?

Peanut butter.
You put it between two slices of bread
for a sandwich.

I don't bother asking for jelly,
because we're trying to save money.

We're standing in line and the checker,
a woman with feathered brown hair,
blue eyes, and blue eye shadow, says to us,
I've seen you all around before.
Are you new in town?

Yes, Ba replies.

I'm Terry.
What are your names?

Ba wants Americans to call him
by our family name, so he says,
My name is Zhang.
This is my wife, Kim,
and our daughter, Anna.

Terry repeats our names,
one by one
and smiles.

No Car

It's been almost three weeks
since we've seen another Chinese person.

Ma longs for friendly, familiar faces.

She reaches out to the small handful of people
she knows in Los Angeles County,
old college classmates and friends of friends.

These people live near the beach
or in a whole other valley,
and I'm beginning to realize
that if Los Angeles County
is one giant octopus blob,
then Duarte is at the very tip
of its weakest tentacle,
small and overlooked.

It wouldn't be so bad if we had a car.
Well, we don't.

Living in Los Angeles without a car means we stay
within the small circle
of school, store, and apartment,
and the distance we can travel by bus.

One of Ma's childhood classmates tells her
about a Chinese church in Pasadena,
only three towns away,
a thirty-minute bus ride
west on Route 66.

Circle

Ba puts on a wool suit.
Ma wears her silk dress
and even I am wearing my nicest skirt.

We ride the bus west toward Pasadena.

Before,
church was a place
where we saw A Gong and A Ma,
our relatives and family friends,
an ever-widening circle of aunties and uncles.

I'd sit through Sunday school,
then run around with the other kids,
while the adults had choir practice.

That's just what we did,
every single week.

I didn't hate going,
but I didn't love it either.

Now I have to admit,
I'd really like to make some friends at this church.
And Ma and Ba,
I think they need some friends too.
It's been just the three of us
for so long.

This One Chance

Four months ago,
that was the last time Ba had a friend.

Right before coming to America,
Ba entered into a partnership
with Liu Fa Quay, his best friend.

Liu had immigrated months before.
He owned a business in LA
selling boom boxes, video cassette recorders,
and other electronics.

Ma said to me,
The day your ba landed in Los Angeles
Liu Fa Quay said to him,
"There's been a misunderstanding.
We're not business partners.
The money you gave me was a loan,
nothing more."

Then Liu Fa Quay tossed him a check, saying,
"Here's your money back."

He took your father to downtown LA
and dropped him off at the Rosslyn Hotel,
a place where you pay for a room
by the week or the month.

Ba waited a day before calling to tell Ma
that the business opportunity that brought him
to the *beautiful country* had evaporated.

What's a businessman without a business?
he said to her on the phone
while I secretly listened in.

Ba wanted to forget everything
and come back.
Ma wanted him to stay.

We only have this one chance, she said.
We have to take it.
My paperwork is almost finished,
and then Ai Shi and I
will be right there with you.

Ba spent the rest of the month
holed up in his room at the Rosslyn Hotel.

And it wasn't until the beginning
of his second month in the beautiful country
that Ba began riding the bus
all over Los Angeles County,
looking for another store to buy.

He looked at a dry cleaners and a Chinese restaurant.
He even considered a gas station.

In the end, Ba settled on Dino's.

Sunday School

We get off the bus and walk
three long blocks to the old, converted house
where the church meets.

They look like us!

It's been so long since I've seen
a sea of black-haired people
with Chinese tumbling out of their mouths.
It's like I'm in Taiwan again.

Miss Chen, the Sunday school teacher,
is kind enough to give us a tour.
She leads us through the meeting space
with its concrete floor and wooden cross.

She shows us the classrooms in the attic,
its closets perfect for hide-and-seek.

There's even a kitchen that's
filled with the smell of steamed rice.

Ma and Ba go to the meeting space
while I go to Sunday school.
And even though there's no guarantee
I'll make friends here,
at least I know the kids won't be mean.
That's the thing with church.
They kind of have to be friendly.

So during Sunday school,
I empty out all the Chinese words
I've stored up this last month.

I've missed talking to kids.

I guess I should have known,
it's like what Ba always says,
You never forget the language of your heart.

American Holiday

The holiday is two words smashed into one,
Thanks and *giving*.

From the pictures I've seen in school,
Thanksgiving has something to do
with Native Americans
and people in black hats called *Pilgrims*.

Ma and Ba decided to close the store
after Mr. Ting from church said,
Nobody will want to eat hamburgers Thursday.

Then he invited us to church and explained,
A lot of us don't have extended family around,
so we have a potluck.

If Mr. Ting hadn't said anything,
we would have worked on Thanksgiving

because we don't know anything
about American holidays.

Now we can have a real day off!

I count on one hand
everything I'm looking forward to.

One,
I'll get to eat some *turkey*,
a very ugly bird that Americans seem to love.

Two,
it's another opportunity to speak Chinese!

Three,
we're closing the store for a day.

Four,
I get to eat yummy food.

Five,
Ma's making one of my favorites, fried shrimp.

I've missed her cooking.

Potluck

It's better than I ever could have imagined.
Chinese food and American food, together!

I go through the potluck line.
There's turkey, of course
potatoes smashed and whipped
and then a brown sauce called *gravy*
to pour over all of it.

There are little bits of cut-up lobster,
swimming in ginger and green onions,
a whole fish, sliced open and steamed,
Ma's shrimp, doused with vinegar and hot chili paste,
sticky rice with shiitake mushrooms for the *stuffing*,
green Jell-O and marshmallow fluff
molded with canned fruit, *Ambrosia salad*,
and apple, pumpkin, and cherry pies for dessert.

For a long time,
there's only the din of forks and chopsticks
and the occasional murmur
of praise for the food.

Everything was wonderful,
only the turkey was a little disappointing,
everyone said, *so dry!*
I had to eat it with
lots of whipped potatoes and gravy.
And even then, only in between
every other bite of pie,
apple, then cherry.

I didn't mind.

Watch and Listen

These days I hear Ba say,
I don't know, so often.

I thought his English
was good and still there's so much
he doesn't understand.

Next to the cash register,
he keeps a thick Chinese-English dictionary.
He flips through its tissue-thin pages
to look up words like *howdy* and *so long*.

Even I know that *howdy* is *hello*
and *so long* is *goodbye*.

Ma knows the least amount of English.
All she can do is watch and try to listen.

Some customers are kind and don't mind
repeating themselves or trying other words.
They smile and start over,
speaking slowly.

Other customers don't like it.
Last week, a man became very huffy and puffy,
as if not understanding English
was some kind of insult.

Sometimes, when I hear angry voices at the store,
I try to find a quiet place.
I go to the back of the kitchen,
behind the refrigerators,
and hide.

Big Mouth

Some kids at school are curious about me
but not in a friendly way.

We're sitting in class watching a film about sharks.
The minute Ms. Branch steps into the hallway,
I hear,
Hey, psst . . .

I look over and it's hay-colored hair, Tammy.

What's your name? she asks.

Anna.

No, your real name.
Your Chinese name.

I think,
Oh! Maybe she wants to be friends
and that's why she's asking.

Zhang Ai Shi.

Tammy's face curls in surprise
and then quickly turns into a snarl.

I see?
Icee, like a Slurpee?

She cackles.

Icee! Icee!
Now she's singing.

I realize I've made a mistake
that's going to fuel days of teasing.
All I can do is stare
into the empty void that is Tammy's big mouth.

I wish I could reach in
and take my name back.

Oak Tree

The other kids save their teasing
for the playground.

And the nice ones,
if you can call them that,
are the ones who ignore me.

During free reading time,
I sit in a beanbag chair next to the window.

I can only read books with three-letter words.
This one is about a cat, a dog, a hat, and Sam.

It's my second-favorite part of school,
sitting by the window,
in the shadow
of the sprawling oak tree, reading.

My favorite part is the swings.

Sunday Afternoon

A day off, sort of.

We arrive back from church
and within minutes,
Ba is lying on the sofa bed,
a blue sheet pulled up to his chin,
snoring.

Ma and I giggle.

A few minutes later, she's asleep too.
Their soft, doughy bodies relax
into the sofa bed, like lumps.

This is the only time I get to be alone.

I go to my room
and look through photo albums.
I try to avoid the birthday photos.

Instead, I look at pictures of my relatives,
photographs of the three of us at the beach,
Ma and Ba's wedding.

Also, there's a picture of Ba from years ago
when he came to California on a business trip.
He's at Disneyland, sitting in a huge teacup.
He's wearing a suit.
I've seen that picture a hundred times.
Only now, I'm in California
looking at a photo of California.
And I know Disneyland is close by,
even though it seems so far away.

I go to the closet and put on Ma's dress,
the one she can no longer fit into,
the one swirled in shades
of pink, peach, coral, and rose.

It doesn't fit me yet
but it's the most beautiful thing I own.
I sit on the floor and look at the light
filtering in through the window.

And I pretend I'm somewhere else,
the California in photographs
and not the California in real life.

I stare out the bedroom window
at the telephone pole,
another tether to my old life,
only a phone call away.

I hear Ma rising from the creaky sofa bed.
Ba is no longer snoring.
I change back into my regular clothes.

It's time to go to work.

Half a Day

Ma and Ba never told me to lie, exactly.
I could just tell,
they didn't want church people to know
we worked on Sundays.

Business is not good
and we need all the money we can make,
even if the store is open
for just half a day on Sundays.

I'm not like the other church kids.
I don't go to Chinese school on Saturdays.
I don't take piano lessons,
and we ride the bus to church
instead of arriving in a car.

Kevin's dad owns a business
importing stuff from China.

Laura's father is a doctor.
Rachel's mom is a scientist
at the Jet Propulsion Laboratory.

We're the only ones who own a store.
Even at church we're different.

Hair

Ma says she doesn't have
the time or the energy
to do my hair.

She says,
I'm not a housewife anymore.

All the other girls at church
wear French braids,
or have their hair curled into ringlets,
or at the very least,
they wear ribbon barrettes.

I have hair that only goes down to my chin,
thick and straight.
When I tell Ma I want ringlets, she asks,
Don't you think they look like sausages?

And even though I was mad,
I couldn't help laughing.

Then Ma said,
I like your hair just the way it is.

She took her hairbrush,
the one I'm not allowed to touch,
and brushed my hair
until it was glossy and soft
and the deepest shade of black.

Pretty Tree

There's another holiday coming up.
I see Santa on soda cans,
on a cardboard display at the Pantry,
on our black-and-white television.

It's a lot of work to keep myself
from wondering if Santa Claus
will show up at the apartment this year.

I'm too old to believe in him.

But even last year,
I was still getting presents *from Santa*.
As if Ma and Ba needed an excuse
to buy a few extra gifts.

I don't think I'm getting anything this year,
not from Ma or Ba or Santa.

We don't even have a Christmas tree.
I save my parents the sadness of explaining
why we don't have one
by not asking.

Before,
we always had a tree,
a plastic one,
almost as tall as Ba,
the biggest among all our neighbors.
It was adorned with silver garland and ornaments,
always a few presents underneath.

When we left,
Ma didn't pack any of the ornaments.
She said we'd buy new ones here.

And it feels so silly to admit,
I miss pretty things.

During art at school,
I take a few sheets
of green construction paper.
I cut, fold, and staple
together

a tree.
I dot the glue
and dust the leaves
with glitter.

I carry my paper tree
from school
to the store,
then back to the apartment,
where I set it down
in the corner of the beige living room.

It's pretty.

I try not to think
so much about before.

Opposites

Always start from the left with the big bills
and work your way to the right.
When all the bills are counted,
gather up the quarters in one hand
and drop them one by one,
back into the cash register,
counting with each clink.
The same with dimes, nickels,
even pennies if there's a lot of them.
Then add everything up.
Eighty-four dollars and thirty-seven cents,
I tell Ba.

I thought he'd be happy
with how I can count so accurately.

He's not.
He's disappointed in the number.

The store is making so much
less than we had hoped.
Ba tells me,
Don't count the money
in the register anymore.
Spend all your time learning English.
You're the reason why we're here,
We came so you could have
a much better life than we ever could.

I didn't know they came here for me.
I thought they wanted to be here for themselves.
I say nothing, except for a quiet *thank you,*
my head bowed, eyes down.

I go to the storeroom to study English.
But instead of studying, I'm stuck
wondering about opposites.
Like a place, can it be both beautiful
and ugly at the same time?
And a person,
can a person feel two different emotions,
can a person be both grateful and sad,
at exactly the same time?

Back Door

At the apartment,
the telephone never rings.
Who would ever call us?

The last person to use the phone was Ma.
A few weeks ago,
she called every Taiwanese person she knew in LA,
asking about churches.

Saturday night,
middle of the night,
the phone rings.

Ba, groggy and half-asleep,
picks it up.
Oh! It's the police.

The store's backdoor lock, broken.
The door wide open,
flapping in the wind.

118

Ma and Ba dress quickly, hurrying off.
They don't want me to come along.

Ma says on her way out,
Just stay here.
Go back to sleep.

I want to run after them,
but Ma and Ba,
they're already gone.

I can't fall back asleep.

Cost of Doing Business

They don't come back
until hours later.
They don't say anything.
Ma and Ba climb back into the sofa bed,
fall asleep.

I guess we won't be going
to church today.

In the afternoon,
they're only half-awake
working in the store.

They're thinking about something else,
so the fries are too brown,
the lettuce is in big chunks.

Every few minutes,
as if she is realizing something

for the very first time, Ma asks,
Who would do something like this?

Ba says,
This kind of stuff just happens.
It's the cost of doing business.

The store's back-door lock cost
fifty dollars to replace.
That's a lot of money
but not horrible.

The person who broke in,
they didn't even take anything.

Adjectives

Sad, sadder, saddest.
Ms. Branch wants me to practice
using these words in a sentence.

There are three people at the store.
One person is sad,
another is sadder,
and the third person is the saddest of them all.

Childhood Home

The store is so quiet it hums.
The refrigerator thrums,
it's the sound of waiting.

Ma gets ready for her nap.
She turns off the overhead lights
and unfolds the lawn chair
we bought at Kmart last week.
She places it behind the two refrigerators,
where she can't be seen.

She lies down,
flings her right arm over her eyes
to block out the light.

If I were to say something to her, she'd say,
I just want to be left alone.

Ba sits at the counter.
I'm next to him and the soda machine.
Now that Ma has been taking naps,
afternoons at the store are for Ba and me.

He tells me about my grandparents,
Zu Fu, Zu Mu.
I've never met them.
Ba left China before the country
closed itself off
and Ba couldn't go back.

At the apartment,
there's only one photo of my grandparents.
Zu Mu is wearing small hoop earrings.
The photo is in black and white
and I can't tell if her earrings are silver or gold.

I've stared and stared at the photo
trying to figure out what her earrings
are made of, silver or gold,
as if knowing would somehow make a difference.

Ba calls his childhood home *lao jia.*
He tells me, *Lao jia means* old home
but it's so much more than that.

I know *lao jia* is where
my grandfather is buried and his father before him.
It's where my family has lived for generations.
It's the place my father longs for.

Lao jia,
that's also where you're from,
he says.

Ba, that's where I'm from?

Yes, it's the Chinese way.
You are from
where your father is from.

It's funny to think of *home*
as a place where I have never been.

Outsiders

But it's more complicated than that.
I'm Chinese and Taiwanese.

Ba's Chinese.
Ma's Taiwanese.
I'm the only one who's both.

Ba doesn't like it when I say *I'm both.*
Ma likes it but she also says, laughing,
Children trace their nationality through their fathers.

It's true, in Taiwan
I was called *wai shen ren,*
an *outsider,*
even though I was born in Taiwan,
because Ba is *wai shen ren.*

Ma says,
If anyone asks about our family,

just say we're Chinese.
I'm outnumbered by you and Ba.
But if anyone asks me directly
where I'm from,
I'll say Taiwanese.

And the kids at school,
who do they say I am?

Chinese, Japanese, Vietnamese,
dirty knees,
that's what they say.

I tell them,
I'm Chinese and Taiwanese.

They reply,
Chinese, Japanese, Taiwanese,
dirty knees.

I thought that here,
the three of us would finally be
the same thing, American.

Instead, we're *outsiders.*

Painted Smiles

It's not just the kids at school.

The people at church are interested
in finding out where we're from.

There's a Shanghainese lady
who wears pearls and red lipstick.
And a lady from Hunan who's short
and doesn't wear any makeup at all.
Then there's a Cantonese woman,
she's somewhere in between.

Ma looks like the lady from Hunan.
Before, she looked like the lady from Shanghai.

What province are you from?
they ask Ma.

Ma tells them Taiwan.
There's a little crack behind their painted smiles.

Ma is the only Taiwanese person here.
I'm only half.

The Taiwanese have their own churches.

Ma tells me,
Actually, a lot of Chinese people
who fled the mainland look down on Taiwan
even though they lived
on the island for years.

Some of them came to Taiwan with families intact.
They moved together as one big unit,
grandparents and parents and children,
while your ba was the only one
of his family to come over.

I ask Ma,
How were those families
able to be all together?

She answers me with her own question,
How do you think?

Uh, money?

She nods to let me know two things,
that I'm right
and that she's done talking.

I'm glad I came up with the right answer.
It's not too hard because whenever
Ma asks me a question nowadays,
the answer is almost always *money.*

Not Like the Others

My homework is different from the other kids'.
Ms. Branch says,
It's just until your English improves.

I get handouts with words and drawings,
so I don't have to know
every single word on the page.

The first question is,
Which of these is not like the others?
car
bus
van
airplane

I look at the pictures next to the words.
The correct answer is *airplane*.
The other three are vehicles with four wheels.

But I want to choose *car*.
In these last two months
I've been on an airplane
and in a van.
I ride the bus every week.

I wish we had a car.

Paperwork

Terry, the grocery store clerk,
is at the store for lunch.

She's emptied out half the contents
of her purse onto the counter.
Here's the paperwork,
and here's the mail,
and oh, there's my wallet.

I'm curious about her,
Terry's friendly and not in a fake way.
When she opens her wallet to pay,
it's stuffed with photos.
I crane my neck to get a better look.

There's a photo of
a man with kind eyes,
his mouth partially hidden by a scraggly beard.

Next to him are two little girls
wearing matching pastel-green dresses.

Terry must have noticed because she says,
Anna, look at this picture of my family.
That's my husband, Don,
and our kids, Tabitha and Sabrina.

Ba's standing right there
but instead of looking at the photo,
he says to Terry,
Paperwork?
I need help with paperwork.
Then he pulls out a letter
sent by the state board last week.

He says he doesn't understand this letter,
even after looking up the words
in the Chinese-English dictionary.

Terry, I can't understand any letter sent
by the government.

She laughs and replies,
That's because it's a special language
called legalese, and even those of us

134

who grew up speaking English
have a hard time with it.

Terry reads the letter while she eats.
She explains every sentence to Ba in plain English,
even when it takes her entire lunch hour.

Christmas Card

I'm thinking about the telephone pole
outside my bedroom window.
Ma still won't let me call Mei,
not even on a holiday.

She tells me,
Phone calls to Taiwan are expensive
and only for emergencies.
Here, you can reread
the Christmas card they sent last week
and write them back.

The store is closed today
and there's not even a potluck.
Christmas is so special,
most church people will travel
to be with their faraway families.
Not us.

We're at the apartment with the blinds drawn
and the television on.
I lie on the floor and reread
all the Christmas cards one more time.
I leave the cards propped up in the corner
next to my construction-paper tree.

One card has a scene of a house
on a cold wintry night,
snow dusting the ground,
candles shining brightly
through every window.
I stare at the card
and imagine I'm inside that house
sitting by a warm, roaring fire.

I pull out a sheet of paper and write,

Dear Mei,
We have a huge Christmas tree
and there are so many wonderful presents underneath.

Two Teenagers

Two teenagers have started coming by.
They pull up in an ugly green car,
blasting loud music.

Nick is the one with yellow hair,
parted in the middle,
feathered on the sides.
Tony has brown hair and pimples.

They spill soda on the floor,
not at all sorry or embarrassed
for making a mess.

They smile big toothy smiles,
glad to have someone else
clean up after them.

What We Can't Talk About

We're going to the New Year's Eve service.
Instead of going back to the apartment,
we'll spend the night at church.

Last week, Mrs. Chiang, the pastor's wife,
extended an invitation.

On New Year's Day,
the Rose Parade is happening two blocks away.
Some church people sleep
in the Sunday school classrooms the night before
and head over to the parade in the morning.

So tonight,
on the last day of 1980,
we close the store a few hours early.

By nine o'clock I'm yawning,
ready to climb into my blankets
sprawled out on the floor of the cedar-lined
closet of the attic classroom.
But some of the other kids,
Kevin and Laura, convince me
to stay up late and play games.

This being church,
there are strict rules about games,
like absolutely *No mahjong*,
because it's associated with gambling.
Checkers is okay, though,
and so is chess.

Mostly, I'm glad for Ma and Ba
that there's this place for them
to chat with other people,
even though there are rules about
which conversation topics are acceptable.
Because in addition to *No mahjong*,
the other big rule is,
No talking about money.

That's probably the most difficult rule of all,
because I think Chinese people

love talking about money.
When I asked Ma about it,
she quoted the pastor, who said,
The love of money
is the root of all kinds of evil.

Then Ma said,
I have to admit,
the pastor has a point.
I mean, look at what happened
between Ba and Liu.

But not talking about money
also means that Ma and Ba
can't tell church people we're really struggling
or that business is no good
or that the person
who sold Ba the store probably lied
about how much money Dino's made,
because how else could you explain the fact
that the store makes so much less
than what the previous owner said it would make?

Also, Ma and Ba don't talk about the break-in
we had two weeks ago
that cost fifty dollars to repair.

They don't say any of those things.

And tonight, even as I see Ma and Ba
drinking tea and eating candied winter melon
with other church people,
I feel lonely for them.

I wish there was someone
they could really talk to.

Part Three

The Year the Locusts Have Eaten

Too Much

I stayed up too late last night,
learning how to play chess.
This morning I had to wake up too early
so we could get a good spot
along the parade route.

The horses were too stinky,
the marching bands too loud.
The parade floats had too many flowers.
The Rose Queen was too pretty.

Also, there was too much laughing and joking
and shouting, *Happy New Year!*

And I loved it all.

Now we're on our way back to Duarte.

The bus lunges and rolls,
and stops in front of Dino's.
I turn to look at the store.

Something's not right.

Squint, tilt my head, look again.

Something's wrong.

Light hits glass wall,
flat.
Black asphalt
sparkles.

Throat
tightens.

Ma and Ba
rush off the bus.

Run! Run!

There's a single
solitary brick
lying

in a sea
of broken glass.

The store's glass wall
shattered.

Nothing Is Missing

The soda machine,
the empty cash register,
refrigerators full of food,
all untouched.

Ma and Ba stare at the hole
where a wall of glass
used to be
and mumble about how
a glass sheet that big
will be very expensive to replace.

Ma says,
It would have been better
if they had stolen some food.
Then at least we'd know
this was done
out of hunger.

They didn't take anything.
They took so much.

Holiday Pay

We wait.

First for the police,
so slow to arrive, then so quick to leave.

Ba gets on the phone again
and speaks to someone from the glass company.

It hurts my ears to hear him talk.
Even I can admit
it's hard to understand his accent
when he's so upset.

Ba's on the phone for a long time.

He doesn't know so many of the words
the man on the other end is saying,
no matter how many times he flips through
the thin pages of his Chinese-English dictionary.

Until finally, Ba understands.
The glass wall cannot be replaced today.

It's New Year's Day.
No one is coming
because of *overtime* and *holiday pay.*

Ba gets on the phone again.

He's speaking to someone else,
someone who can board up
the wall with plywood,
so the store doesn't have
a big gaping hole.

Then the long wait
for that person to show up.

And Ba murmurs under his breath,
to anyone who happens to be listening,
How many hamburgers
will I have to sell
to pay for all of this?

Plywood

We go back to the apartment.
It is already dark.

It cost a hundred dollars
to board up the wall with plywood,
a hundred dollars
we don't have.

The sheet of glass will cost so much more.

And we realize, this could keep happening.
There could be another break-in
and another pane of shattered glass,
again.

I'm hungry, but Ma and Ba
are not thinking about food.

Ma lies down on the sofa bed,
flings her right arm over her face,
and falls asleep.

She doesn't get up
until the next morning
when Ba shakes her shoulder.

It's time to go to work.

Ma gets up slowly,
as if she's being held back
by a heavy heart.

I feel like my heart is sinking too.

When Good Things Happen

Before,
when I was lucky,
I always had this feeling deep down
that I got away with something
and that next time,
my luck would turn.

I guess what I really believe
is when good things happen,
bad is just right around the corner.

On New Year's Day I was too happy
and look at what happened.

And for most of my life,
I've been lucky.
I've had a long string of good days.

Now I'm scared of all the bad
that's up ahead.

Quicksand

Now that the big gaping hole is boarded up,
Ba's not in a hurry to replace it.
He's worried about how much it will cost.

Every time I look at the front of the store,
I get the same sinking feeling
I had on New Year's Day.
It's like I'm a cartoon character
stuck in quicksand
and I can't get out,
no matter how hard I try.

Only for me,
the quicksand is around my heart.

Against Code

We're used to the front of the store
no longer being so bright.

Ba says,
Maybe we won't replace the glass
and just leave the plywood in place,
as it is.

Ma asks,
And if they break another glass wall?

Then we'll board that up too,
all the way around until the store is
shielded in plywood.

Before that happens,
the city sends over
the health inspector to tell us,

You can't leave the wall boarded up.
It's against code.

And Ba doesn't know what
the guy means by *against code.*

I don't know either, so
we look it up.

The dictionary states,
Code is a system of words,
letters, figures, or other symbols
substituted for other words or letters or symbols
especially for the purpose of secrecy.

Then we read the second definition,
a systematic collection of laws or regulations.

Code can either be a secret language
or a collection of rules,
or both.

The glass replacement guys come by
three days later.

The front of the store is bright again.

Witness

The two teenagers, Nick and Tony,
like to come by in the afternoons.

Sometimes, they'll just sit
in the parking lot in a Ford Pinto.

They only like to come in
when there are no other customers around.
That way they can be rude
without any witnesses.

We witness their rudeness, of course.
But I guess we don't count.

Today, they make fun of Ba's accent,
asking for an order of *flies*
instead of *fries*.

And they laugh and laugh,
full-bellied and hateful.

Translation

My English is so much better than Ma's.
I'm the one who translates for her
when Ba's not around.

Last week, when he went to the bank,
it was just Ma and me at the store.
A customer came in
and Ma couldn't understand
what the customer was saying.

He thought that by repeating himself
over and over again,
each time a bit louder,
Ma would understand.

She didn't.
It just made her even more embarrassed.
I'm sorry, she said.

I hid behind the refrigerators.
I could tell by the tone of her voice,
she was hunched over,
her entire body an apology.

Ai Shi! Ai Shi!
She called for me.

Yeah, Ma?
Please help.

I stepped out,
and turned toward the customer,
Can I help you?
even though I knew exactly
what it was he wanted.

I want the food in separate bags,
he yelled.

Yes, sir,
I replied.

I translated for Ma.
She nodded and smiled
and put the man's food into separate bags.

The customer walked to the door.
He already had his hand
on the door handle and was about to leave
when he decided to turn around and say,
You should learn English
if you're going to be in this country.

Then he let the door swing shut.

Ma asked,
What did he say?

Oh nothing,
I lied.

Trade Stories

There's one customer
who comes in the afternoons,
when the store is not so busy.

He has gray eyes,
dry skin the color of worn leather,
and when he's not eating,
drinking, or smoking,
there's a toothpick forever
dangling out of the corner of his mouth.

Richard orders something cheap, like fries,
and takes his time eating.
He pecks at the food,
maybe because his teeth are no good
or maybe because
he can't really afford anything else
and needs to make the fries last like a meal.

Richard likes to talk.
So does Ba.
The two of them trade stories.
Ba talks about sailing the world on a cargo ship.
Richard talks about being a horse jockey.

When they chat,
Ma goes to the kitchen
and naps on the Kmart lawn chair,
while I sit with them
and take it all in,
until I know their stories
like I know my own.

It's been a long time since
I've thought of the stories
I used to tell myself,
the ones that ended with *happily ever after.*

Bad Luck

Richard's limp is worse today.
He says it's because of the rain.

Richard used to race horses
at the Santa Anita racetrack,
just five miles down the road.
That was until he was thrown
from a horse,
hopes dashed,
right leg crushed.

All his stories center around that accident.
Now Richard works as a stable hand,
taking care of rich people's horses.

He says,
I was almost famous,
but that fall was the beginning of the end.

Real bad luck.
You know what I mean?

Ba takes a swig of Dr Pepper
before replying,
I know what you mean.

Good Money

Ma and Ba fight
whenever they are around each other.

They are around each other
all the time.

Ma says she's afraid the break-ins
will not stop.
I'm afraid too.

The store is a sinkhole.
We're throwing good money after bad,
she keeps saying.

Ba comes up with a solution.
He will sleep at the store every night
to keep watch.

Ma begs him not to.
What if the vandals find you and beat you up?
We'll be even worse off.

Ba is not convinced.
I can't sit around and do nothing.
I either sleep at the store
or stay at the apartment and not sleep at all.

I think it's a great idea.
I want to sleep at the store too.
But Ba won't let me.
He says, *It's something*
I have to do alone, duckling.

Ba walks the two blocks back to the store
to spend the night there.

Levi's Jeans

Kids have not teased me
about my lunch in a while.
There's nothing funny
about a peanut butter sandwich.

Now they're making fun of my clothes.
Rodney, the boy in my class
who makes slit eyes,
keeps talking about a *flood*.
He points to my pants.
Where's the flood?

I don't know where or what the *flood* is.
After school, I ask Ba.
He thumbs through the dictionary
and reads the definition to me,
an overflow of water on dry land.

Oh, I get it.

Rodney was teasing about my pants
being too short,
stopping above my ankles.

I'd find it funny too,
if I wasn't the one being laughed at.
I've grown so fast.
The ruffled shirts are too tight.
The corduroy pants with patches
of embroidered flowers are starting to creep up.

Ma hands me a large garbage bag
of old clothes gifted
by someone from church.
I pull out a pair of jeans,
so soft and long.
There are two more pairs just like it.

I pull out a red shirt.
It has little pictures of cars and trucks all over.
There's the exact same shirt in yellow
and another one in blue.

Shirts with pictures of cars and trucks?
I hate them.

I don't say anything to Ma and Ba,
even though my parents
are giving me boys' clothes to wear.
Because it would be worse
to say something,
only to have them reply,
We don't have enough money
to buy you new clothes.

If I had a choice,
I'd buy a collection of T-shirts
in a whole array of colors.
Then when I dressed in the mornings,
I'd pick a color based on my mood.
Blue if I was sad.
Yellow for energetic.
Pink if I wanted to feel pretty.
For pants, I'd buy blue jeans
just like the ones out of the garbage bag.

They're called *Levi's*
and look exactly like
what all the other kids are wearing.

No Hobbies

We're assigned to the same group
to talk about our hobbies.
Rodney says he plays baseball.
Kelly shares about Girl Scouts.

I tell them I don't have any hobbies.

Then Amy says,
Aw, come on,
I bet they make you play the piano.

No.

I don't have all the English words to answer.
Otherwise, I'd tell them,
I used to play the piano and hated it.
My teacher would tap my fingers
with a ruler whenever I made a mistake.

Amy asks,
What do you do?

This time I have all the words,
so I say,
I work at my parents' store.
They own a fast-food place.

Then Rodney says,
Ugh, that's why you smell like hamburgers.

Everyone at the table laughs.
Now I remember why
I don't like attention.

American Friend

Today, Ba and Richard talk for a while
before Richard says,
I'm a little low on money.
How about if you give me some food today
and I'll pay you back next month?
It's called a tab.

Ma doesn't think it's a good idea,
but she leaves it up to Ba.
Ever since Liu, she's been saying,
We shouldn't let money get mixed up in a friendship.

Ba doesn't want to say no to a friend,
so he agrees.
That's what Ba calls Richard,
my American friend.

Red Shirt

There's another new year coming up,
Lunar New Year.

There's nothing to celebrate,
no one will be handing out red envelopes.
We are not having dumplings, steamed fish,
eight treasures sweet rice.

Yet Ba still encourages me to wear red.
He says,
Red is a lucky color.

I don't believe wearing a certain color
will make a difference,
but I put on my red cars and trucks shirt
because Ba asked me to.
Then do what I usually do.
I hide it under my zipped-up jacket.

I remember last year,
we celebrated Lunar New Year
with A Gong and A Ma, aunts, uncles, cousins,
over thirty of us gathered in Ma's hometown,
the place where her family has lived for generations.

I couldn't walk down the street
without some stranger
recognizing me and saying,
Aren't you Kiem's daughter?
Last New Year's was when Ma
announced to our relatives,
We're immigrating to the beautiful country.

All the adults were sitting
around the dinner table,
their mouths glistening
with the sweetness of rice cakes.

One by one, the adults
toasted to our good fortune.
How lucky you are!
How lucky!

I remember sitting at a table with my cousins.
I didn't look at Mei.
I didn't want her to feel bad,

so I kept my head down,
to hide my happiness.

That was last year,
when we were considered the lucky ones.

What I wouldn't give
to celebrate Lunar New Year
somewhere else, anywhere else,
but here.

Tonight,
I take off that red shirt
and stuff it in the back of the closet.

I don't want to wear it ever again.

Another Friend Gone

Richard owes us money.
We haven't seen him for a while now.

Ma waits a few more days before saying,
I don't think Richard is ever going
to pay us back.

Ba shrugs.

It's not so much the money.
It's the loss of the friendship that hurts.

Another friend gone.

And because I sat around
listening to so many of Richard's stories,
he felt like my friend too.

Split

Now in the afternoons,
each of us goes
to our own little part of the store.

Ma gets the kitchen for nap time.
Ba sits at the counter,
next to the cash register.
I go hide in the back storeroom.

I climb onto a shelf
and pull out from the velvet purse
my old lip balm tinted pink
and the few coins I've received
from customers for wiping down tables.
I look at the shiny quarters and dimes,
wishing they could multiply.

I reach for the letter that came
in the mail last week from Mei,

the one I've already read three times.
I read it again.

Her letter is about the Lunar New Year,
about getting a week off from school.
She writes about her new clothes
and the get-togethers with relatives.

There's even a picture of my four aunts,
a thin sliver of space left blank
where Ma used to stand, in between
Auntie number two and Auntie number four.

I miss seeing their faces,
but it would have been better
if she had not sent any photos at all.

I remember the last time
I was at Mei's house,
and the thought I had about our lives
splitting into two separate paths.

I see what my life
would have been like
if we'd never left.

I wish Ba and Ma never became
businesspeople and we had just stayed.

And I wish I was a girl
who didn't know anything about break-ins
or working in a store
or being different from everyone else in school.

We're not so lucky after all.

Passive Voice

Ms. Branch tells us,
You want to use active verbs.
You want the subjects of your sentences
to do things,
rather than have things
done to them.

Now you try.

I write,
She yells.
He ran.

A mistake was made.

Empty Heart Vegetable

Ba wasn't the only one
who wanted a friend.
Ma too.

Ma called Liu Fa Quay's wife,
the woman married to Ba's old business partner.
Ma and Mrs. Liu were friends too,
before everything blew up.

Ma called her and said,
We're all Christians.
Let's not let money get in the way of friendship.
Please come over to the store for a meal
and let's put the past behind us.

Ma wears a white eyelet dress
even though she's working.
It's the first time she's put rollers

in her hair since forever,
and she's wearing red lipstick too.
She looks like she did before.

Liu Fa Quay and his wife
drive up in their fancy Lincoln Continental.

Ma serves them ribs and fried chicken strips,
rice, stir-fried *kong xin cai*,
which is *empty heart vegetable*,
and soup.

Mrs. Liu looks at the plates of food
and wrinkles her nose.
She puts one chicken strip on her plate
and takes a big heap of *kong xin cai*.

Ma points to the ribs and asks,
Would you like one?
It's the store's specialty.
We just made a big batch of sauce today.

Mrs. Liu replies,
I don't gnaw on ribs
like a dog.

The way she spit out those words
felt like a slap in the face.

After they left, Ma said,
The Lius look down on us
because they think
people will be buying boom boxes
and videocassette recorders
for the next hundred years.

Then Ba said,
Yeah, but they rent their store.
We own Dino's and the land.

I felt bad because owning an electronics store
seems a lot nicer than owning Dino's,
even if they are renters.
Besides, they'll be in business
for the next hundred years.

I think Ma felt bad too.
After the Lius left,
Ma spent a long time in the bathroom
changing back into her work clothes.
When she finally came out,
her eyes were red and puffy
from crying.

Scar

Ma says the ladies from church are friendly,
but they're not friends.

Otherwise, why hasn't anyone extended an invitation
for a visit or a meal?
Even though we don't talk about money at church,
they can still ask,
"How are you?"

The fancy church ladies notice
the burn marks on Ma's hands.
In front of all the other women,
Mrs. Wang pointed and asked,
What happened?

Ma said,
Oh, it's nothing.
That's just what happens when you work
over a griddle all day.

Then she looked at each of the women
until they looked away first.

During the church service,
Ma kept staring at the cross
while touching her scar-worn hands.
She seemed strangely at peace.

Two Scoops

Terry, the grocery store clerk
with the blue eyes and blue eye shadow,
comes in for a late lunch
while we're eating our family meal.

Now that Richard no longer comes around,
the afternoons are quiet again.

Terry sees us with our bowls of rice and says,
I love rice!
Can I have that
instead of a bread roll with my order?

Ba's about to tell Terry,
Sorry, rice is not on the menu,
when Ma stops him.

Ma puts two scoops
onto Terry's plate and says,
I hope you enjoy.

Living Room Again

Today when Terry comes in,
Ma has a bowl of rice waiting for her.

Five minutes later,
a man with smiling eyes
and a furry beard walks in.
He has two little girls with him.

I recognize them right away
from the photo in Terry's wallet.

Terry says,
This is my husband Don.
And Tabitha, she's five.
And Sabrina, she's four.

Don says,
Terry tells me the food's real good here,
so I had to come try it for myself.

This makes Ma so happy
and she's off to pick
the meatiest, juiciest ribs for Don's plate.

After all the food is prepared
and the Eatons settle down at a table,
the three of us
go our separate ways again.

Ma's in the kitchen for her nap
and Ba sits at his usual spot next to the cash register.

I park myself behind the counter
and pretend to write in my notebook.
I know it's not nice to eavesdrop
but I can't help it.

I like being around a family that's nice to each other.
It's been so long since the store has felt like
a living room.

Alliteration

We're learning about poetry.

In class
Ms. Branch says,
And the silken sad uncertain rustling.

On the playground,
Rodney says,
Ching Chong Chinaman.

Sticky Mess

Nick and Tony are here again,
It's starting to be like clockwork,
every Wednesday.

Nick shakes salt on his fries.
It lands on the table, chair, floor,
everywhere
except his fries.

Tony takes the lid off his soda cup
and leaves a sticky mess.

Nick and Tony are like two little kids.
Our store is their playground.

Superpower

Ms. Branch asks the class,
Would you rather be invisible
or have the gift of flight?
Which is the better superpower?

If I chose flight,
I could go anywhere I want
and help people.
I could fly sick people to the hospital
faster than it takes for an ambulance
to drive there.

I could even go visit relatives in Taiwan.

If I chose invisibility,
I could hide in plain sight.
No more teasing.
Nothing.

I choose invisibility.

Personal Space

Even though I don't want to be seen,
I see everything.

Like the way Terry and Don talk to the girls
during their dinners at the store.
Americans don't tell their kids
the sort of things Ma tells me.

She doesn't just talk about
how much the store makes every day.
I know how much money is in the bank
and how much money
they will need to take out
of the savings account this month.

I know why Ma holds off paying
the electricity bill until the very last day.
She tells me about how much rent
costs for the apartment.

She says I need to know these things
because I'm getting older.
But I think it's because she has no one else to talk to.

You're no longer a child, she says.
I'm telling you this so you understand
how difficult life can be.

She's right, I'm not a child.
But sometimes, I'm the one
who has to look out for her
because there's so much she doesn't know.

She doesn't understand
how Americans love *personal space*
and how if you inch your way
closer and closer
to the person in front of you
in the checkout line,
the woman will eventually turn,
smile, and say, *Excuse me.*

Except it's not a real smile
and she doesn't mean *excuse me,*
she means *excuse you,*
and what she really wants
is for you to step back.

But you don't know any of that.

So even though I'm much too old
to be holding hands, I do it.
I put my hand in yours
and gently pull you
a step back from the lady
in front of us,
because you don't even know
how to stand in line
at the supermarket
anymore.

If-Then

Ms. Branch stands by the chalkboard and says,
If you eat nothing but candy,
then what's the logical conclusion?
You will get sick.

Now, who has an if-then statement to share?

I have an if-then statement,
but it's not shareable.

If Rodney keeps bullying me,
then one day I'm going to lose it.

Reflection

Today, when we're supposed to
have a time of quiet reflection
at the end of Sunday school,
I try something different.

I list a series of if-then statements
I've been thinking about
ever since Ms. Branch's class lesson.

If the break-ins cease,
If Nick and Tony stop bothering us,
If Rodney quits picking on me,
If the store starts to make money,

Then,
I will never ask for another thing.

I have good practice.

There's this little hole in my right shoe,
and I've developed a habit of tucking in
my foot when sitting.
That way, Ma won't notice
and have to buy me a new pair of shoes.

Slim to None

Yesterday early morning, a Saturday,
Ba woke to the sound of breaking glass
and the screech of tires.

He was asleep in the storeroom
and came out to find a single lonely brick.

When Ma and I walked to the store,
Ba had already cleaned up.
He told us,
I won't be sleeping at the store anymore.

He didn't even bother calling the police.
Last time, all the policeman said was,
Vandalism's on the rise.
The chance of catching
whoever did this is slim to none.

And Ba didn't know what *slim to none* meant.
I had to tell him,
It means there's almost no chance.

The front of the store is dark again.

Trouble

Ba does not refuse to serve them
even though they make such a mess.

He doesn't want trouble and besides,
we need all the customers we can get,
even if Nick and Tony
are only buying soda and fries.

When Nick and Tony are here,
it doesn't even feel like
it's our store anymore.
It feels like they've taken over completely.

But after Nick and Tony
start squirting ketchup
on the table for fun,
Ba tells them to leave.
Get out!

They get up.
Nick kicks over a chair.
Tony, with one hand on the door,
turns and says,
It's too bad about the glass.

His eyes are smiling
even before his mouth curls into a smirk.

That's when we knew.

International Calls
Are Very Expensive

Ma calls Auntie,
Mei's mom,
to borrow money
for a new glass wall.

Equal Weight

Ma wants to stay.

Ba's the one who wants to go back,
and yet he's also the one
who told me years ago,
when I barely knew
anything about nations and borders,
Taiwan's not a country.

And I asked him,
How could the country where I was born
not be considered a country?

That's when Ba told me
about the United Nations,
how in 1971,
they called a meeting
and with all their members assembled,

took a vote to strip
Taiwan of its nation status.

I was two years old
when that happened.
So for as long as I've known,
Taiwan is my birthplace,
I've also known,
Taiwan is not a country.

I've lived in the middle
of these two statements,
of equal weight,
this whole time.

Other Life

They can hardly talk without fighting,
so she talks to me.

Ma says there are some things that
Ba just cannot talk about.

She says,
I want you to know why
your father is the way he is.
He's lived a whole other life before us.

I know this is true.
Ba's thirteen years older than Ma.

And there are whole swaths of his life
that she knows nothing about.
But what she does know,
she repeats

over and over
to make up for his silence.

Ba talks about his *lao jia,*
but he never talks about leaving home.

In Ma's telling and retelling,
his story has become her story.
And it's mine too.

She tells me,
As a young man, your father went to Taiwan
to attend the naval academy.
He was only supposed to be there
for a year, at most.

But when the war between the Nationalists
and the Communists broke out in full force,
your father couldn't go back.
So there he was,
alone in Taiwan.

People would say to your father,
"You were so lucky to get out."

He didn't feel lucky.
Your father was all alone.
Everyone he had ever loved was in China.
The only connection he had to family
was through the slow trickle of letters
that took weeks to route.

It was through a letter
that your father learned
of his father's death.
And then a few years later,
his mother's death.
Of course, he didn't attend the funerals.

There was a chasm between Taiwan and China
that could not be crossed.

And besides,
by the time he received the letters,
several weeks later,
he was already reading about the past.

It was only when he had given up
hope of returning to China,
that your father finally married.

Now you understand why your father
wants to go back.
Even though Taiwan is not his home,
your father is tired.

He's already lived a whole other life
before us.

Small, Smaller, Smallest

Ma and Ba have been trying out a new rule.
No fighting at the store.

Today they break that rule.

It starts out quietly,
their voices murmuring,
until her voice rises
and his falls silent.

Ma yells about
the break-ins,
the money that still needs to be repaid,
what a mistake it was to trust Liu,
what a mistake it was to trust Dino's previous owner.

Ba says,
I'm not interested in arguing about the past.

Ma takes off her apron,
walks out the door.

I call after her.

She doesn't turn around.
She keeps walking west on Route 66,
small, smaller, smallest,
then disappears.

Wanderer

We close the store
and walk back to the apartment.

He asks,
Have I ever told you why
I wanted to come to the beautiful country?

I reply,
Economic prosperity, freedom,
a better future for me,
and also, Taiwan's not even a country.
I have these words memorized.

That's what I used to say,
but none of those are the real reason.
The truth is, I have been looking for a place
to call home for a long time.

I left China right before
the Communists came into power.
That was when I left the only home
I ever knew.
And since then,
I've been a restless wanderer.

I thought this place
could become home
but it's not.
I was not at home in Taiwan,
and I'm not at home here.

When your ma comes back,
I'm going to tell her,
she can decide if we stay
or go back.

Either way,
my home is with the two of you.

Box

Ba lets me stay up late watching TV,
while we wait for Ma to come back.

She will come back.
There's nowhere else for her to go.

I stare at the television,
this little box that sits inside
the bigger box of our living room.

Sometimes,
I just want to climb inside
and live there
even if that world is black and white.

Sinking

I dream about a swimming pool full of water.

Ba and Ma are standing beside me
throwing paper towels into the pool.
They take turns tossing one sheet at a time.

I ask Ba,
What are you doing?

He tells me,
I'm trying to soak up the water
with paper towels.

Ba, that will take forever.

Yes, I know,
he says, laughing.

I wake up screaming about paper towels.

Ma is kneeling beside me,
smoothing away the loose strands of hair
clinging to my forehead.

Shh, everything's all right.
You had a nightmare.

Oh, Ma's back.
I knew she'd be back.

Then I remember what is dream
and what is reality.
I feel like I'm sinking.
It's the same feeling I had on New Year's Day,
my heart in quicksand.

Nothing, no one
can help me
get out.

Prayer

They don't talk anymore.
The only thing
they do together is pray.

Even then,
their prayer is
only a few words.

They sit
and stare
at the distant mountain.

God,
give us back
the year
the locusts
have eaten.

Shadow

In the mornings
when I go to school,
I walk toward the mountain.

And when I arrive,
I'm not any closer.

The mountain does not move.
It is certain,
fixed,
and I am so small
in its shadow.

Not Enough

Zhang Ai Shi, come here and sit down.
There's something we want to tell you.

I know it's serious
when they use my full name.

We're in the kitchen,
hidden from the front of the store.
I sit on the lawn chair
Ma uses for afternoon naps.

We've decided to move back.

What?

Ma's voice quivers.
We've been throwing money into this sinkhole
and the break-ins are just too much.
We can't make it here.

Her shoulders slump forward.
After all the weeks of arguing,
they finally decided.

What about the store? I ask.

Ba says,
We'll sell the store
and when we go back,
I'll get a job.

But what if you can't sell the store?

We'll have to see.

He doesn't look at me.
His back is straight as a rod.

I want to ask,
What about all the hopes you had
for a better life?
What about finding a place to call home?

But I don't say any of this.
Instead, I say,
So we're just going to go back?
That's it?

I'm looking at Ba,
but it's Ma who replies.

There's nothing wrong with going back.
It's not as if we're bad people.
It's not as if we're not smart enough
or not hardworking enough.
It's just bad luck.

There's a lump in my throat
that won't go away,
no matter how much I swallow.
I keep swallowing to stop myself from saying
what I'm really thinking.

I wish we never came here.
I wish we never heard of
the beautiful country.

Paths

It's not that I don't want to go back.
I do.
I miss my relatives and friends
and my old life.

But what would we even be going back to?
I don't even know where we'd live.
Our old house is gone.
Ba's old job is gone.

And if we sold the store at a loss,
there would be so much money to repay.

If we do go back,
what does that make Ma and Ba,
failed *business owners*?
It hurts to think of them that way.

I imagine what it would be like,
sitting around the table,
the first family dinner with relatives
after our return.

I picture Ba sitting with my uncles.
There would be this awkward silence.
Ba would have to say something like,
Oh, it just didn't work out.

And the look on Mei's face,
a weird mix of sadness and satisfaction.
She would be the lucky one,
not me.

Our paths are so far apart now.

Don't Cry

End of the school day,
the din of a hundred voices all talking at once
and the sound of sneakers on pavement
behind me.

I walk fast.
They walk faster.
Hey, hamburger girl!
out of Rodney's big mouth.

I'm not fast enough.

He's blocking the gate.

I can't get through.

There's three of them
and only one of me.

Quick breaths,
scared
to open my mouth.

Afraid
that anything I say
will sound wrong.

Don't cry.

Rodney's hands
pull at his eyes,
slits.

ching chong,
ling long,
ting tong.

Tears blur.
I can't see so well.

Good.
I don't want to see
his face.

Don't cry.

It takes all
my concentration
to keep the tears
from spilling.
I bite the inside
of my cheek.

Please,
don't blink.
If you blink,
tears will fall
and then you'll
have lost,
because he made
you cry.

Oh, I blinked.

I'm sorry.

So many
tears.

He made me cry.

I hate him!

Shove
Punch
Scream

Leave me alone!

No more laughing.
No more *ching chong*.

Feet scamper away.

It's so quiet.

I'm all alone.

Not Alone

Ba is the first one to see my face,
flushed and stained with tears.

What happened, duckling?

His arms open wide.
I feel the warmth
of his breath on my hair.

I tell him about hitting Rodney.
I can barely get the words out
without crying again.

I tell him the whole story.

And in the telling,
it's as if I'm right there at school again,
so scared and angry.

Only this time,
Ba is beside me
and I'm not so alone anymore.

Ba says,
I'm proud of you, duckling.
Sometimes you have to fight.

Ba has this faraway look
as he wipes the tears off my face.

Numbers

When I walk back from school,
Ma and Ba are sitting at the corner table
with a Chinese man.

Ba asks,
What do you think?

The Chinese man uses silence like a tool.
He takes a gulp of soda
before replying,
It's hard to say.
Show me the ledger.

It's only then I realize,
they're talking about the store.

Ba shakes his head,
hangs his head low.

The ledger will show that
the business barely makes any money.
But the land is worth . . .

This time the man doesn't wait at all.
He cuts Ba off, saying,
Well, if the business is not even profitable,
then it could take a very long time.
Unless you're willing to make the numbers
look a little better than they actually are,
it could take forever . . .

Now it's Ba turn to cut him off.
Ba says,
We're not willing to do that.

And the man leaves.

Ma tells me later,
the man is a *Realtor*
who goes to our church
and that when he said,
make the numbers look better
than they actually are,
he meant creating a fake ledger
so the store would appear profitable.

At church, I see the Realtor
sitting in the first row,
looking so satisfied with himself.

It's pretty much understood
that the front pews
are reserved for the truly deserving.

Less

Now that we're planning on going back
as soon as the store sells,
I no longer look at the stuff
in our apartment
and think,
So little.

Now I think,
Too much.
I wonder if we will go back
with less than we came with.

Yes, I think we will leave with less.

American Dirt

Their conversations start
and end the same way.

The Realtor will say,
No one's going to buy this place
if it doesn't show a profit.
Don't think of it as lying.
It's called injecting a little optimism.
Everybody does it.

Then Ba will reply,
Yes, everybody does it.
That's how I was tricked into buying
this store in the first place.
I thought it was profitable
and I trusted the guy
who sold it to me.
I'm not going to put anyone else

through the misery I've been through.
Besides, even if the business isn't valuable,
there's always the land.
This is one hundred percent American dirt.

Then the Realtor gets up
and leaves his plate on the table,
what's left of the free meal
he eats every time he's here.

For the rest of the afternoon,
you'd think there would be
a lot of yelling,
and talk about all *the mistakes that were made.*
But they are quiet with each other,
sitting side by side,
staring at the mountain.

Ma and Ba are united on this one point.
They don't want to cheat
anyone else
in the same way
they've been cheated.

One Man

Today, before Nick and Tony come in,
Ba's standing outside
blocking the front door.
You cannot come in!
Get away!

They call him
Chink, Jap, Gook,
then sit in the parking lot
blasting heavy metal music
from the Pinto before taking off.

Terry's sitting at the corner table by herself,
watching all of this.
She asks Ba,
Who are those guys?

Starting from the very beginning,
Ba tells her everything,

about how Nick and Tony
have been coming into the store
to cause trouble for a while now,
and how we think they're
the ones responsible for the break-ins,
and how we're trying to sell the store
because we just can't take it anymore.

Then Terry says,
Zhang, I'm so sorry
about all you've gone through.
I'm going to talk to Don about this.

Terry, you can talk to Don,
but what can one man do?

And she just smiles and says,
Oh, you'd be surprised.

A Little Conversation

Wednesdays,
I've trained myself to look out for Nick's car.

It's the one day we can count
on Nick and Tony coming around.

Ba! They're here.

Last week Ba didn't get to the door in time.
Even though Ba refused to serve them,
Nick and Tony sat around for half an hour,
marking up the table with a pen.

Today, they walk in,
don't even pretend to order anything.

I walk toward the back,
to get away from the quicksand.

But then I hear the door jingling
and the steps of sturdy work boots.

Hey there, Zhang!

I know that voice.
I run to the front.

Don!

Hi, Anna!
Zhang, these the guys
you were telling me about?

Ba nods.

Don walks over to Nick and Tony
and grabs two fistfuls of T-shirt,
AC/DC and Iron Maiden.

Guys, let's go outside for a little conversation.

Tony's no longer smiling.
Nick is forced to stand up so quickly,
his feathered blond hair flaps
like the wings of a bird.

Outside, Don lines them up against
the store's glass wall.
He's inches from Tony's face, yelling.
Why have you been picking on this family?
Don grabs him by the shoulders and shakes.
It doesn't feel so good, does it, being bullied?

Don wraps his hand
around the back of Nick's neck.
You are never to come around again.
And if there's another break-in,
I'm gonna find you
and make you pay.
Now get out of here!

Don takes a step back.
His face is soft and calm again.

The two teenagers run
like little kids,
tripping over their feet along the way.

Waiting

Ba, tell me again,
how did Don know when to come?

I told him Nick and Tony
usually come on Wednesdays.

So Don was just waiting
in the parking lot for them to show up?

Yes, he was sitting in his car waiting.

Umbrella

The day after
Don yelled at Nick and Tony
and they scurried away,
I felt something had lifted.

I don't know if they
will ever come around again.
Or if there will ever be another break-in.

I don't know
if we'll be able to sell the store.

But I don't feel so afraid anymore.

It's as if
before,
we were caught
in a torrent of wind and rain.

Terry and Don walk by,
carrying a huge umbrella.
They wave us over,
Come stand here with us.

We found shelter from the storm.

Sleepover

Saturday morning, the three of us are standing
in Terry's checkout line
even though it's the longest.

Hiya, Zhangs!
I was thinking,
how about Anna comes over
to our house for a sleepover next weekend?

Ba doesn't understand.
He asks,
Pardon? What is an over sleep?

Terry laughs,
You know, Zhang,
a slumber party, a pajama party!

Ba's still stumped.
A slumber party?

Yes! I take Anna to my house for the weekend.
That way you guys can get a little break.

I know all about slumber parties
from overhearing the girls at school.
Of course, I've never been invited to one.

Ba replies,
We only let our daughter
stay with family members.

Well then, call me Aunt Terry!

I love how Terry has an answer for everything.
I really want to go.

Ma's gently elbowing Ba to translate.
Before he can get out the last word,
Ma and I are both nodding and smiling,
Yes! Yes!

Weekend

I'm trying not to dart my eyes around so much.
I can't help it.

It's been so long since
I've been inside someone else's house.

There's a sparkly crystal vase
and a cabinet with teacups
and these red-cheeked figurines.
Terry calls them *Hummels*.

I want to run my fingers
along the lace tablecloth,
so I sit on my hands.

Terry asks,
What should we do this weekend?

Before anyone has a chance to answer,
she opens a white box,
nudges it toward me.
Want one?

Inside are chocolates,
each in brown ruffled paper, like little skirts,
See's Candies.

Thank you.

I bite into a squish of caramel and marshmallow.
I sit there chewing and wondering
if all Americans keep boxes of candy
in their living rooms,
just waiting to be eaten.

Terry keeps talking about the weekend.
I'm only half listening.

I know, let's go to Disneyland!

I almost choke on a wad of caramel and marshmallow.

Oh!
There's no way
she just said what I think I heard.

Except Tabitha and Sabrina
are jumping up and down, screaming,
Disneyland! Disneyland!

I keep chewing.
I know Disneyland is somewhere around here.
Even though lately, it's been hard to believe
the happiest place on earth is nearby.

Months ago, I asked Ba if we could go.
He replied,
That place is no fun when
you have to take the bus there and back.
And that was the end of the discussion.

It's only after I'm certain
Terry didn't misspeak that I say,
Aunt Terry, that's wonderful!

I allow myself to feel a little happy,
even though a part of me knows
it's not quite right,
going to Disneyland for the first time
without Ma and Ba.

Dreaming

When it's time for bed,
I'm on a trundle
in Tabitha and Sabrina's room.

I can't fall asleep right away,
so I lie there staring at photographs
of their relatives on the wall,
looking for the same kindness
I find in Terry's and Don's faces.

For the first time in a long time,
I am not worried about the store or Ma and Ba.

I fall asleep dreaming about
the happiest place on earth.

Forgetting

The best part is the forgetting.

I forget about the store.

I'm just a kid,
with other kids.

We eat corn dogs, turkey legs,
cotton candy, pineapple whip,
frozen bananas.

I crane my head around,
my eyes big from looking,
especially during the ride
It's a Small World.

It's okay to be small here.

And Don, somewhere between
Frontierland and Tomorrowland,
became Uncle Don.

Maybe it was when he offered
to carry my jacket,
or maybe it was when
he bought Tabitha, Sabrina, and me
matching Minnie Mouse T-shirts.

We left Disneyland just as night started to fall.

I sank into the car, exhausted.
It was a good kind of tired,
the kind of tiredness
that comes from too much happiness.

Seen

Was it all a dream?

No, I can still feel the sun shining
on my face from the day before.

I get up and make my way to the kitchen.

Good morning!
You want some breakfast?

Yes, please.

Tabitha and Sabrina scoot past on their way
to watch television.

Breakfast is one of three boxes,
Lucky Charms, Cocoa Rice Krispies, or Kix.

I sit down and pour
Lucky Charms into the bowl,
then a splash of milk.
The plan is when I finish off
the very last pastel marshmallow,
I'll have the Cocoa Rice Krispies next.
Then Kix.

Sunlight floods the yellow kitchen.

Terry's hands are wrapped around a mug of coffee,
steam rises up like a halo above her face.

I ask,
Why did you take me there?

To Disneyland, you mean?

Yes.

*Because I wanted to give you
one day
where you could just
be a kid.*

Container

It seems like so long ago.
It was only last week.

One fun day
in a string of sad days.

Everything else was the same.
Ma and Ba still so worried about money
and the store
and the Realtor finding a buyer.

The day after Disneyland,
Terry dropped me off at the apartment
and I wondered,
What difference does a day make?

Nothing and everything.

Disneyland was just one day.
But the memory of that day stays with me.

I wish I could take all that happiness
and put it into some sort of container,
something I can hold on to
forever.

Then I realize,
I am that container.

Part Four
Home

Half-Truth

I spend every day of summer
working at the store with Ma and Ba.

Before school let out,
the kids went around the room
and shared about summer plans.
They talked about camps,
and family vacations,
and visits to Grandma's house.

I said very little because I'd learned
my lesson about sharing too much,
or to borrow a phrase I heard in Sunday school,
Don't throw pearls before swine.

I really wanted to say,
So long, suckers!
Instead, I told them

I'd be traveling to see family,
which was a half-truth.
Because when we finally sell the store,
we are going to visit relatives.
We'll just never come back.

And even though
I felt glad to be done
with Royal Oaks Elementary,
I was sad about what I would miss:
my kind teacher, Ms. Branch,
the tree outside the classroom window
that had become a reading companion,
and the swing
that gifted me with
both flight and invisibility.

Summer

There's one good thing about summer.
It's quiet.

We have not seen Nick and Tony
since that day three months ago
when Don told them to leave us alone.
And we have not had another break-in.

Ba's finally been sleeping through the night.
He's no longer on the edge of sleep,
half expecting to be woken up
by a ringing telephone,
with the police on the other line.

At night, Ba lies down on the sofa bed.
Five minutes later,
he's snoring like a baby.

Ma's starting to cook again,
and I mean good food,
not just throwing a bunch of meat
and vegetables into a pot
and boiling until ten minutes shy of mushy.

Still the Realtor has not found a buyer.
Ma and Ba insist they won't sell the store at a loss.

Instead of saying *when we go back*,
now they've been saying *if we go back*.

Secret

First day of school.
I can't believe I'm still here.

I plop myself down in the middle
of an empty table.
I don't want to eat lunch by myself anymore.
I'm sick of trying to be invisible.

The other day, Ma said,
The secret to making friends
is not to care so much
about what other people think.

Then just yesterday she said,
The secret to getting people to like you
is to like yourself.

I just rolled my eyes and said,
I'm not sure where you're getting

these fortune cookie sayings.
And we laughed.

But then I thought about it and she's right.
I don't want to care so much
about what other kids think.

And if no one wants to be my friend,
well, it's their loss.
Besides, I'm wearing nice long Levi's
and lunch is two pieces of white bread
with a big clump of Skippy peanut butter in between.
There's even jelly in it.

Tiffany, the new girl with red hair,
sits down across from me,
a little to the left.
I've never seen anyone with red hair before.
She starts to say something.
I hold my breath.

I have a peanut butter sandwich.
What's yours?

Peanut butter.

Creamy or crunchy?

Creamy.

Lucky!
I wish I had creamy.

Lucky.
It's been a while
since I've heard that word.

Free Lunch

I still don't know if we're staying or going.
The Realtor keeps coming around
once a week to give us an update.
But really, he just wants a free lunch.

He says to Ma and Ba,
You have to either adjust the ledger
or lower the price.

Ba says he'll think about it.
I already know what Ba thinks.
If we lower the price for Dino's,
we'll end up selling at a loss,
and we can't do that.
Because then we won't have a store
and we'll still owe my aunts money.

And Ba's already made it clear
he's not willing to lie on the ledger.

I don't even know why the Realtor doesn't
just give Ma and Ba an update
when they see each other on Sundays at church.

Oh right, I forgot,
it's because there are rules
against talking about money at church.

But it's okay for him to freeload
a meal off us every week?

What a jerk!

Small Drop

It's been three and a half months
since we've seen Nick and Tony.

Until today.

Our usual Saturday morning trip
to the Pantry,
I turn the corner,
and there's Nick
pushing a wheelchair in the cereal aisle.

The woman in the wheelchair looks just like him.
She must be his mother,
even though she looks too old
to be his mother.

Her right arm is twisted and gnarled.
She holds it close to her body.

Nick's hand adjusts the blanket
that wants to slip off her shoulder.

I can't help but stare.

I'm not staring at the woman
so much as at Nick,
who looks like a good son,
pushing the creaky wheelchair
at such a slow, steady pace.

I feel a twinge of sadness for him
and for this woman who doesn't look well.

It's a small drop of sadness
that disappears
into an ocean of hate.

Fresh off the Boat

There's a new family at church.

Laura, the other sixth grader,
says they're *fresh off the boat.*

The girl, she wears these pants
that are way too short.

We're standing around,
waiting for Sunday school to start,
so I say,
knowing she won't understand,
Hey, are you wearing high-waters
'cause you're fresh off the boat?

Kevin busts out laughing.
Good one!

272

My face flushes with pride
and only a little bit of shame.
I couldn't resist.
Besides, the girl doesn't understand.
She doesn't speak a lick of English.

But then I see the look on her face
and it's strangely familiar.

Now Miss Chen says it's time
for the Sunday school lesson.
She drones on
and I'm not really paying attention.
But then I hear the words,
We all need forgiveness.
We all need to forgive.

And for the first time in a long time,
I'm listening.

I realize
I was mean to the new girl
because I wanted so bad to be
funny and cute and clever.
I haven't been any of those things
in a long time.

And I think about all the people
who have hurt me,
Rodney and Nick and Tony.

Maybe Nick was mean to us
because he didn't know what to do
with the ocean of hurt
in his own life.

I understand a little better now.
But I don't know
what to do with this knowledge.

I don't know how any of us
will ever be able to get off
this never-ending merry-go-round
of hurt and hate.

Hundred Little Pieces

When we get back from church,
I pull out a sheet of paper,
make a list of
all the people I'm angry at:

Nick and Tony,
Liu,
Richard,
Dino's previous owner,
the Realtor.

The kids
who teased me about my lunch
and my clothes
and my name.
Rodney,
who did all those things.

And the kids who stood by and said nothing.

The people at church
who looked down on us for being poor.

I sit and stare at the list.

Then I write,
Ma and Ba,
for being such bad businesspeople.

And Ba for saying months ago,
we came to the beautiful country for you,
so you could have a much better life
than we ever could.

Lately I've been wanting to tell Ba,
I never asked to come here.
It was your dream, not mine.

I stare at the list for a long time.

Then I tear it up
into a hundred little pieces.

Never Let Go

That new family from church
is coming over for dinner tomorrow.

Ma tells me to be nice to the girl,
the one with the short pants.

I'm still embarrassed
about being mean to the new girl.
I ask Ma,
Why are we having them over?
No one from church
has ever invited us to their house.

Ma doesn't say anything,
which is a bad sign.
When Ma gets quiet,
that's when she's really mad.
So I tiptoe around to look at her

out of the corner of my eye.
She doesn't look too angry, just serious.

Oh phew.

Ma says,
We've had a hard time here, haven't we?
It hasn't been as easy as we thought.
Our only friends have been
a grocery store clerk and her husband.

I can choose to be bitter,
but I don't want to let goodness
be overshadowed by evil.

Ai Shi,
if there's one thing
I want you to learn, it's this:
hold on to what is good.

With all your strength,
grab hold of the good
in this world
and never let go.

Corner Table

Ma didn't even sleep this afternoon.
She spent nap time
preparing food for tonight's dinner.

We're gathered around the corner table,
our first time having people over.

There's stir-fried chicken with peanuts and chili,
black pepper beef and greens,
steamed fish with ginger,
green onion pancakes,
and a soup of clear chicken broth
with snow peas and bamboo shoots.
Hot grass jelly with taro
and sweet rice dumplings for dessert.

The girl, her name is Wen Han.
Her brother is Jin Ai.

After dinner, the adults linger
over chrysanthemum tea
and dessert.

I tell Wen Han and Jin Ai,
I have some advice
that will make your life easier.

You probably already know this,
but don't bring rice to school for lunch.
Pack something between two slices of bread,
like peanut butter,
or this meat called baloney.
It's not so bad with a lot of mustard.

For clothes, don't wear stuff from China
with misspelled English words on it.
If you have nothing else to wear,
then just keep your jacket zipped up all day.
Also, make sure your pants go all the way
down to the top of your shoe.

It takes all my willpower not to glance
at Wen Han's pants.

Before I can say anything else,
it's time for them to go.
I lean over and whisper
one last piece of advice.

*Tell your parents they should
let you watch a lot of TV.
Tell them that's how I learned English so quickly.
There's this one show on Saturday night
that's pretty funny.
It's called* Love Boat.

Kind

Afternoons,
instead of going to the storage room,
I'm starting to sit next to Ba again
by the front counter.

Today,
a man we've never seen before
walks in and asks for a hamburger.
He says he'll pay for it tomorrow.

I don't have any money,
he says.

I'm standing behind Ba,
waiting for him to say no,
waiting for him to tell the man,
Get out.

Instead, Ba says, *Okay.*

He goes to make a hamburger.
I follow after Ba, whispering,
What are you doing?
That man is not going to pay us back.

He's not, is he?
That's all right.
That man's hungry and I have food.
I don't mind being kind.

All Three

I keep thinking of Ba's kindness,
how he fed the stranger
who was hungry.

I think about the words Ma said last week.
I turn them over in my head,
again and again.
Hold on to what is good.

And then there's what Miss Chen said
in that Sunday school lesson
about forgiveness.
Let go of unforgiveness.

Be kind.
Hold on.
Let go.

I want to do all three.

Jump

I run into Nick again at the Pantry.

I'm staring at a box of Froot Loops
just as he turns the corner.

I settle my eyes on the woman
in the creaky old wheelchair
before turning away.

A part of me still wants to hate him.

I remember the way his face looked
when he called Ba a *Chink*.
I remember the sea of broken glass
and the way my heart
was smothered in quicksand
on New Year's Day.

But it's not about feelings.
It's about getting off this never-ending
merry-go-round.

I jump.

If We Stay

Instead of *if we go back*,
it's now, *if we stay*.

No one has made an offer on Dino's.

Ba says,
The decision is being made for us.
If there's no buyer, then we stay.
Besides, now that the break-ins have stopped,
it's not so bad.

Ma says,
Maybe this place can make money after all.

I don't know if I can get used to the two of them
agreeing with each other
more often than not.

Today during lunch,
Tiffany, the new girl, says,
I hope you don't move.
I wait a moment before replying,
I want what's best for my family.

I know that's a weird answer
because you're supposed to know what you want.
But I just want Ma and Ba to be happy,
and I'll figure out my own happiness later.

I think about Taiwan
and the certainty
that awaits us
if we go back.

I think about our life here
and the uncertainty
that remains.

Either way,
we're not nice, straight lines.
We're three crooked,
zigzagging lines.

I'm starting to be okay with that.

Extra Large

Ma and Ba want to add items to the store's menu.

I suggest,
The extra-large drink!

Ma and Ba don't think it's such a good idea,
but I insist.

Americans love big soda cups!
Lots of people will ask for the biggest size
without even thinking about it,
and then we'll make
an extra ten cents right there.

Ba says we can give it a try.
He orders a sleeve of big cups.
He makes a sign on poster board,
tapes it up next to the soda machine.

Cold and Refreshing!
Extra-Large Soda!

Pork Sung Sandwich

Ba makes egg sandwiches for me
when we're out of peanut butter.
I'm not so upset about it.
I like fried eggs.
Sometimes I even ask for my favorite,
pork sung in between two slices of bread.

Tiffany sits down at her usual spot.
We've been having lunch together ever since
the first day of school.
After lunch, we'll either play tetherball
or go on the swings
or walk around the open field, talking.

Today, she asks,
What kind of sandwich is that?

The filling is called pork sung.

Oh, can I try?

I hesitate.
I'm afraid Tiffany's going to say something
really horrible about my sandwich
and then we'll stop being friends.

But then I remember what Ma said.
The secret to making friends is not to care
so much about what other people think.
I break off a bit of my sandwich
and hand it to her.

She takes a bite,
wrinkles her nose, and says,
It's so fluffy
like, like . . . carpet.

In my head, I'm thinking,
Oh, I've made a big mistake.

But Tiffany keeps talking.

The meat is really soft.
I like it!
A carpet sandwich, ha!

She's smiling and there's no hint
of meanness at all.

So I join right in.
Carpet sandwich sounds pretty good to me!
I'll vacuum one up right now.

We cannot stop laughing.

Five Spice

This morning I wake to the smell of orange peels
and chrysanthemum tea
left over from the night before.

Ma's been tinkering with the store's
barbecue sauce recipe.

She takes cinnamon, clove,
pink peppercorn, fennel seed, star anise
and adds soy sauce, sugar, ginger for
five-spice barbecue ribs.
The ribs are spicy, sticky, sweet.

Ma's been giving Terry and Don
plates of free food for being taste-testers.

Don says,
These are even better than regular ribs!

Terry says,
It's so delicious,
I want an extra scoop of rice
to soak up all the sauce.

I'm proud of Ma.
She's smart about running a business
and her English is improving.

Ba says that since Ma came up with the recipe,
we should pick a name that honors her.
He tapes a sheet of poster board on the glass wall.

Special! Special!
Taiwanese Five-Spice Ribs!

Ledger

The left column is the date.
The right column is income.

This is a real ledger, not a fake one.

At night,
Ba writes in the number,
how much the store made that day,
and adds it to the other numbers.

Before,
when Ba would add up all the numbers,
he'd just close the ledger and sigh.

Today he doesn't close the ledger right away.
He sits and looks over the page again,
admiring the numbers.

How It Goes

Noon on Saturday,
the Realtor arrives just in time for lunch.

He likes to eat first, then
tell us how hard he's tried to
find a buyer for Dino's.

Today, Ba doesn't even wait
for the Realtor to say anything.

Ba tells him,
We've decided we don't want to sell.
Please take Dino's off the market.

You think that's a good idea?
the Realtor asks.

Well, business has been picking up.
We're going to see how it goes.

All right, let me know if you change your mind.
The Realtor buttons up his suit jacket,
gets up to leave.

We will.
And that will be $3.59 for lunch.

Steady Stream

Just like Terry, other customers are asking for rice.
There are more people buying
five-spice ribs than hamburgers.
Ma adds fried rice to the menu
only after days of testing the recipe.

She tells us,
I want to make something
that's both Taiwanese and American.
She adds soy sauce, *too salty!*
Oyster sauce, *too fishy!*
Something's missing.
She tries ketchup.
That's it! A blend of sour, salty, sweet.

Ma's forehead is smooth these days.
It's the edges of her eyes that are crinkly,
from smiling at the steady stream of customers.

Ask

Tiffany and I are sitting
next to each other on the swings.

She asks,
When's your birthday?

In a few weeks.

Oh, you should have a party.

I wasn't planning on it.
Last year, it was just the three of us, one donut,
one single candle.
I don't tell Tiffany any of this.
Instead, I say,
I don't think I can.
The apartment is too small.

The week before,
I went to Tiffany's birthday party.
We had pizza and played games in her backyard.
Pin the tail on the donkey.
Horseshoes.

I try to change the subject.
I ask if she's ever seen a jar of Goobers.
It's peanut butter and jelly in one jar, together!

Tiffany won't let it go.
You should have it at the store.

What?

You should have a birthday party at the store.

Where would we play games?

The parking lot.

What about food?

Are you kidding?
Isn't there plenty of food at the store?

I tell her I'll think about it.
The truth is a part of me
doesn't want to ask Ma and Ba,
even though they've been telling me,
Ask for what you want.

It's still hard not to feel like
I'm being a bother.

Second Halloween

One year.
That's how long we've been here.

In three days,
it will be Halloween.

My first Halloween,
I didn't know anything.
I didn't know why a ghost child
came to our door.

Now I know she was saying,
Trick or treat!
and all she wanted was some candy.

This year,
I'll be the one going door to door
with Tiffany and her mom.

I'll be the one in a white sheet,
shouting, *Trick or treat*,
asking for candy.

Paper Bag

I wake up to find a white bag
and a card with the words
Happy Birthday!
in Ma's handwriting.

Inside there's a blouse,
purple lace and silk,
puffy sleeves,
buttons as shiny as pearls.

There's no label.
The blouse is not from a store
and it's not a hand-me-down.

Ma must have made this with the sewing machine
we bought at the thrift shop last month.
She sewed at night
after I'd already fallen asleep,
so it would be a surprise.

I glance over at Ma's old dress
hanging in the closet,
the one I would wear for dress-up.
That dress is no longer
the most beautiful thing I own.

The blouse is too nice for school
but Ma encourages me to wear it.
She says,
You look so pretty.

And it makes her happy to see me happy.

Twelve Candles

I've invited all the girls in my class.
I didn't want anyone to feel left out.
Besides, I'm willing to be friends
with anyone who wants to be my friend.

Tiffany and six of my classmates are coming.
Terry and Don and the girls are stopping by.

Ba and I buy fourteen rainbow-sprinkle donuts.
We stack them on a plate in layers,
top it with twelve candles.
Ba takes a picture.

When the guests arrive,
I stand by the soda machine
and fill drink orders, one by one.

Ma passes around plates
of five-spice ribs and fried rice.

We play one game,
pin the tail on the donkey,
then run around
tossing water balloons in the parking lot.

At the end of the party,
one of the girls, Melanie, says,
You're so lucky
your parents own a restaurant.
It must be so fun to work here.

I wait a moment before replying,
Yeah, I'm pretty lucky.

Oranges and Chrysanthemum Tea

November,
the store's best month ever.

Ba says business is picking up
with all the money coming in
from the five-spice ribs,
fried rice, and extra-large drinks.

It looks like we just might make it.

The apartment smells like oranges
and chrysanthemum tea all the time.
Ma and Ba are thinking about the future again,
just like before.

Yesterday, at closing time,
they talked about getting a bigger apartment,
and buying a car
and visiting the Grand Canyon someday.

Then I heard Ba say,
in the middle of their conversation,
Enough talking.
Time to go home.

It was the first time
Ba has ever called this place *home.*

That was when I realized,
I've been calling this place
home for a while now.

Acknowledgments

I heard a rumor once that book-making people are some of the kindest, most sincere folks one could ever hope to meet, and I'm happy to report it's true.

Thank you, Alexandra Cooper. You're a brilliant editor.

Thank you, Jennifer Laughran, agent extraordinaire. You believed in my story from the very beginning.

Thank you, Allison Weintraub, for being kind and sending along well wishes for a great weekend whenever I emailed on a Thursday or Friday.

My gratitude to all the HarperCollins professionals who worked on this book: Lindsay Wagner, Valerie Shea, Rye White, Gwen Morton, Meghan Pettit, Allison Brown, David Curtis, Erin Fitzsimmons, Delaney Heisterkamp, Lauren Levite, Patty Rosati, Mimi Rankin, Katie Dutton, and Rosemary Brosnan.

Thank you, Julia Kuo, for the gorgeous cover art.

Thank you, Gene Luen Yang, for the amazing book blurb.

Thank you to my generous and kind first readers: Sally Fung, June Park John, Eric Johnson, Susan Van Riesen, Anna Van Riesen, Michael Chang, Susi Jensen, Henry Tsai, and Yale Ogburn.

Thank you, Mindy Chiang, for your Mandarin expertise.
Thank you, Yangsze Choo, for the advice.
Thank you, Julie Li, for all the ideas and encouragement.

Thank you to the Feedback Loop Meetup: Jenni, Patrick, Filomena, Maryam, Ellen, Alice, Jeff, and Mitch.

Thank you to the writers' group hosted by Gail and Bob Kaku: Harry Cutts, Pamela Chang, and Andrew Lee.

Thank you to the teachers and editors who encouraged me along the way: Caroline Goodwin, Marcy Weydemuller, Monica Wesolowska, and especially Jeannette Larson and Roberto Lovato.

Thank you to the supportive community of writers in the South Bay Writers' Group, especially poets Mia Malhotra and Iris Law, who taught me how to honor my writing.

Thank you to my sister Linda for the love and support.

Thank you, Ma, for all the love and advice.

Dad, I love you and miss you.

My sons Joey and Nathan, thank you for being mine.

My husband Jon, thank you for believing even when I doubted. I love you.

To the Creator who has always loved me, thank you for this beautiful world.